Moondust

Cleveland W. Gibson

Hadrosaur
LBF Books

Cover Design: Laura Givens

Interior Illustrations: Laura Givens

Edited by: Jacqueline Druga-Johnston

LIC in Progress

A co-publication of:
LBF Books, Pittsburgh, PA
&
Hadrosaur Productions, Las Cruces, NM

www.lbfbooks.com

ISBN: 1-885093-42-X

FIRST PRINTING

Acknowledgements

My wife Rosamund and son Michael for their patience in watching this book take shape. Mrs Laura Gibson, my mother, for doing everything to help.

So many people have played an important part in helping me to make this book happen. I offer my deepest thanks to:

John and Jenny Lee, Gill Scholes, RD Larson, Tony Robinson, Mike Broemmel, Frances Rove, Larry Nicholls, Laura Hird, Neil Marr and Cait Meyers. All have given me support, help and encouragement.

Tricia, Footsteps to Oxford and Laura Hird for their useful help and publicity.

Gerry Hughes, creator of Acrebury, (All Rights Reserved), for his help to span the world of sound.

Friends at East of the Web including Rebecca and those at Zoetrope including Diane, for enthusiastic feedback and criticism.

Jacqueline Druga-Johnston of LBF Books for offering me this chance to be published.

Jenny Hewitt for editorial assistance and suggestions. Gillian Nott for her extra editorial flair.

Teresa Tunaley, editorial art director, for making the project happen.

Laura Givens for her wonderful illustrations and imagination.

Plus many other friends who have played a part in helping me write this book.

Cleveland W. Gibson
Faringdon, Oxon
August 2005

Moondust

Cleveland W. Gibson

To John and Jenny
Moondust —
— it's all true!
Cleveland W. Gibson

The Trophy Room

"Incurably insane, me? Never, Doctor Leo Harper! I was clever enough to kill my best friend and get away with it.

"Guilty? Ha! Let me tell you this was not murder. Yes; a mystery, perhaps, in the best Sherlock Holmes tradition, but judge for yourself.

"I was in a locked room. Sure, I emptied my rifle, but where did all the bullets go? Three people said they heard screaming, yet I was alone. The room was full of smoke and smelt of burning flesh, but forensic experts confirmed nothing had been burnt. Intrigued? Just give me five minutes. Let me prove to you I am both sane and innocent."

Peter Cosford stopped for a moment and I caught him looking at my tall and very athletic figure. I always reasoned my hours in the gym paid dividends. It was at a road race at Bristol that I met Diana. We married and had two girls. At thirty-two years of age I guess I was in the mood to settle down and be happy. I tried to ignore how my hair had already started to thin.

He was an inmate at the Chinnereth Mental Institute, where I worked as a psychiatrist. I knew him to be extremely intelligent, but more than a little strange. I guess there's the rub. I kept a wealth of information about him because he was my patient.

I noticed he was ordinary looking, his hair shot with grey and nothing in his manner to suggest he was unhinged. His blue eyes, however, seemed a little wild today, and a curious twitch had developed on his right cheek.

I had spent a lot of time in the past interviewing him, coming to the conclusion although he might be normal, something in his psyche made his behaviour unstable. I knew he could be a threat to society. Now here he was offering to disclose all the facts about his case. His motives for doing so intrigued me.

The Chinnereth Institute in Swindon was famous for its

notorious inmates. In a cell behind me was a patient who had poisoned his family, and just across the corridor was a vicious child killer. As this is my diary, I guess I am allowed to say, with tongue in cheek, that I was certainly keeping good company.

Peter rolled back the sleeves of his shirt. I noticed the tattoo of St. George on one arm, and the dragon on the other. England's patron saint held his sword in the famous St. George parry, and the mystical dragon spread its wings in glorious colours. I knew at once the tattoos were special to him; dragons often guarded treasures, even those locked in the subconscious mind.

"It all began in my army days in India," Peter said, "when I was ordered to pick up my friend James Walton. Seems he was good at this undercover game, going native and all that. I knew he was involved in breaking up drug rings and some strange illegal secret societies. Colonel Digby Carruthers, at Army Headquarters Calcutta, ordered me to find Walton immediately although it meant blowing his cover.

"I arrived at the village Mijar but couldn't locate James, so we stopped overnight. Suddenly in the early hours of the morning I heard a terrific scream from the hut James had shared with his Indian helper, Ali Hakki. I was first out with my revolver.

"Inside the hut I saw a large crocodile. It had ripped off Ali's arm and was crunching up his head. Blood dripped from massive jaws as it stood there looking at me. I was scared, but had to do something. I shot it and watched in amazement as it rolled over and died without a struggle.

"Next morning, I coaxed some info out of the headman. Apparently, the same croc had attacked people on a nearby riverbank some days ago. James had disappeared at about the same time. I immediately instigated a search, but without any luck. James had vanished."

"Tell me what was this crocodile like? I'm really interested."

"It was big, a magnificent beast, so on an impulse I had it stuffed and sent back to my family home in Faringdon, Oxfordshire. I placed it in my trophy room where the walls were covered with mounted animal heads, drakki drums, Zulu spears and shields from Upper Volta. And now the crocodile took pride of place in the trophy room.

"Years later, after I returned to civilian life in Faringdon, a cardboard box arrived from James's married sister, Sarah. In her letter she explained she was going to live in Canada and wondered if I'd like her brother's old papers and notes.

"I found them intriguing to read; James was brilliant in many ways; languages, science, music and art. His pen and ink sketches impressed me so much, I took a couple to a tattooist and had them copied onto my arms.

"In amongst his effects, I read some notes on how he'd paid a fakir for a particular secret. This secret would enable him to change from a man into an animal, a skill he hoped to use in his undercover work.

"I was gripped, nay intrigued, by the legend and instructions in red ink: 'White bottle first, then blue'.

"I was puzzled until I discovered two white bottles and two blue bottles in the box. I cast my mind back to those days in India...to the time when James vanished and the crocodile appeared. Using lateral thinking prompted me to conclude that James and the croc were one. Hell! Was I right? Had Ali panicked and not used the blue bottle on him because the sight of the enormous croc terrified him? Would the same croc walk three miles from the river just to kill him? A homicidal croc? I don't know but I remember the strange look in its eye when I shot it. Why? Did it recognize me? The questions were endless."

"I think you are asking me to believe quite a lot of...junk. Surely what you've said didn't really happen. But carry on with your intriguing story." I scratched my chin as I continued listening to Peter Cosford.

"Suddenly, I felt unable to resist the compulsion to climb the stairs to the door leading to my trophy room. I was apprehensive as I entered. I looked around. Sweat burst out on my face and hands because I did not know what to expect.

"I saw the familiar crocodile. By its side I saw a little blue bottle. I was terrified -- I knew the bottles were still in the cardboard box downstairs where I'd left them.

"When I saw the blue bottle, I accepted this as part of my destiny. I picked it up and poured the contents over the croc. At first, nothing seemed to happen. Then I heard a sound which started miles away, yet quickly filled the room. From a gentle whispering, like dry leaves being swept along by light breezes, the sound developed to such an intensity it made me think of daemons as I could not compare it with anything else. As the sound reached a crescendo, James appeared lying on the table in front of me.

"He was a mess; his body was bleeding, he'd lost fingers, and his face was covered in bruises. Around his head hung a wreath of stinking weeds. Leeches clung to his body, drinking his blood.

"Before I could run, his arm shot out. I felt his hand tighten on mine with a grip of steel as he dragged his face closer to mine. I looked into his bloodshot eyes. He croaked: "Burn me, Peter. Let me rest! It's the only way."

"Good God! What did you feel when he made that request?"

"Well, I didn't feel scared any more; just sorry for a friend I'd lost. I had to help him. I snatched up my hunting rifle, but though I shot him at point-blank range, the bullets were useless. He didn't belong to this world anymore.

"Before he could grab me again, I rushed off and found some fire-lighters. I struck a match and soon had a fire going. As the flames licked his body he screamed again and again, the smoke filling the room. About two minutes later James was reduced to a pile of grey ash.

"A new worry emerged as I heard police sirens and cars in the stable-yard below. Boots were already thudding up the stairs as I secured the door.

"As I turned I had a shock. I saw a white bottle on the table right next to the ashes. I gulped and, snatching the bottle up, sprinkled the contents on to the ashes. The stuffed croc was back. It looked menacing. Nothing had changed.

"When the police forced the door they could not find a body, yet those who had heard the screams and reported in, claimed a murder was committed. The room was full of smoke and everyone could smell flesh burning, but if they were right, just what was burning? Nobody could answer the question or the puzzle of my hunting rifle. Forensic tests showed I had emptied the weapon but no bullets were to be found in the trophy room.

"The Thames Valley Police carted me off to prison and the trial made the mass media. But as nobody believed a word of my story, I ended up here in this loony bin. Okay, okay. I killed, but the police couldn't pin this on me. They explained everything by saying I was mad.

"Now, Doctor Leo Harper, do you believe me?"

"Well, it is interesting," I replied, "but tell me how you hope to support your claim? What proof do you have to show me your story is true?"

"Easy. This is my proof. It's all I need." He passed me a small white bottle. "Keep it and give it a try. Don't worry, the bottle will work. When you see the strange reaction for yourself you will believe I am normal."

Peter started scratching the tattoo of the dragon on his arm. He waited for me to reply, but I only looked at the dragon. So mystical, with fascinating colours simply out of this world.

"Well, I enjoyed the yarn. There is certainly plenty to think about. Thanks again." I left the Institute clutching the small white bottle.

For some strange reason the tattoo of the dragon was always in my waking thoughts.

Days later, I remembered the white bottle, and tried it out on our ginger cat. As I did something huge and leathery exploded in front of me. It knocked me down on my knees and I felt a hot rush of wind. My hair was scorched and my hands were blistered. For seconds I was dazed, and then I saw the dragon as I got to my feet; already a black dot in the sky with flames and smoke trailing behind it. I'd never seen a creature like that before except, I guess, on Peter's arm as a tattoo. Instinctively I sensed evil and prayers tripped off my lips...I hoped it wasn't too late.

My suspicions were confirmed when the local radio station told of a fierce flame-spouting dragon swooping on crowds in Swindon's shopping Parade. There were also reports of the dragon eating sheep in nearby Wroughton. The worst incident happened when the dragon burst through the plastic dome of the Oasis Leisure Centre at North Star to snatch a swimmer.

The army sent in the SAS, equipped to fight a mini-war, but still the dragon eluded them, and it was apparent from the television pictures the beast was growing in strength and size each day. Naturally I felt guilty because I had unleashed such a fiendish monster on the world. I knew for every dragon there must be a champion like St. George who could slay it. But such a hero is hard to find, and I needed someone like him to save England.

As more people died, my conscience dictated I confess all to the police. As a doctor I could explain how the incident had happened... until the irony struck me. They...the police...they would never believe me just as I hadn't believed Peter Cosford. I guess I would have to keep my mouth shut even as the death toll mounted.

Over the weeks, after its first appearance, the beast killed hundreds of people. The frightened public voiced their fears to their Members of Parliament. I too felt concerned as I read the papers and followed every news item. The dragon incidents reported on television attracted a vast audience. Viewing figures jumped by millions even as foreign television crews relayed the terrifying news about the dragon back to their country.

"Something needs to be done," the leader of the opposition party told the Prime Minister. "And right now."

As the army formulated plans the dragon attacked those in the steel clad John Murray building in Swindon's shopping complex. Quickly the surprise news broke concerning the trapped dragon. The opportunity to kill the beast forced the army to react swiftly.

The SAS company, picked to tackle the dragon in Swindon, arrived and maintained a low profile. In order to help the soldiers limber up for the battle, the government forced a complete media ban. 'D' notices appeared everywhere, as the public were evacuated and steel barriers erected.

Within minutes of entrapment the dragon thrashed around in an attempt to escape. The security forces moved quickly on to the next phase of their plan. They positioned a large crane alongside the building and suspended a tough plastic sheet from it for privacy. Then, as the official photographers clicked their cameras, the SAS attacked.

The first rockets struck the dragon and the sound of its agony deafened those near by. More explosive shells blasted into the dragon and started phosphorus fires. Wave after wave of missiles followed but still the dragon raged. Clearly to kill the dragon an assault of major proportion needed to be made.

For one hour the attack on the dragon stopped as the troops arranged explosives underneath the lift in which the dragon was trapped. It took an intensive effort to pack eighteen tons of explosives around the base of the lift.

Eventually the soldiers withdrew and the world held its breath as a masked SAS officer gave the signal. The explosion that resulted shattered every pane of glass in the John Murray building. Great cracks appeared in the sides and bare metal showed through in places as masonry crashed to the ground. Clouds of dust filled the air. Minutes later came the secondary explosion accompanied by the loud cry of agony from the beast. The cry got weaker until even that ended. The dragon died. I couldn't help but be reminded of the 911 disaster in America.

The media reported as much of the incident as allowed. I watched countless interviews with staff from the Armoury at Leeds and the weapons experts from The Royal Military College of Science at Shrivenham. The public, it seemed, maintained an insatiable appetite for dragon related news.

I watched many discussions on TV as people speculated on where the dragon might have come from. I knew and bit my lip, as I thought hard. When Britain counted its dead my insides churned every time I saw photos of the victims. I was stunned when I learnt seven hundred people had died in the dragon attacks. The total shocked me. I watched the television screen, so filled with remorse I wanted to confess all. It was only by a supreme effort I remained silent in the hope people would forget and the memory of this all would fade away one day.

Pity, I told my wife, though, 'cause she blabbed out everything to the police. So now Her Majesty takes care of me for the rest of my life, as I play cards with Peter Cosford and talk about dragons and little white bottles.

Dragon Man

"Dr Massey speaking. How can I help?" Brian said. His work as a psychologist at the Hammond Institute meant he often answered the phone. It was after one a.m. and the call, at such an early hour, surprised him.

"Brian. It's me, Larry." the piteous voice croaked. Brian recognised the caller as his father-in-law, Larry Stephens but he sounded so strange, so very tense. Jan, his wife, often stayed the night at Larry's place, so he wondered what had happened?

"Calm down and tell me what's wrong. I'm here to help, remember? It's my job. Is Jan all right? It's just you sound so bad," Brian said. "Come on, loosen up, Larry."

"We've lost her - Jan's dead." Larry's reply made Brian pause as he gasped in disbelief. He gripped the phone tightly. Then he flooded Larry with questions, but didn't get the answers he wanted quickly enough. Something had blown Larry's mind to put him in deep shock.

"She screamed again and again. God! I wish I'd been faster. I grabbed my old revolver and rushed to her bedroom - the door was open. In an instant, I saw it standing by her bed - something black and sort of leathery. It was small but growing every second, and it seemed to have wings that shimmered down its back. And then came the flames. All I could do was empty my gun and run. I've managed to close the door but it's trying to get in. Hear it? Jan's dead – I've rung the police. I'm scared. I can't stand it. Sorry, Brian."

In the background, Brian heard police sirens. In seconds the door shattered with a resounding crash, followed by a mixture of grunts and groans. Somewhere in the gurgling, the rasping, the muffled screams, Brian recognised Larry's last struggle and his cry before the flames engulfed him. In listening, Brian felt numb; it was enough to make him shiver. Then the line went dead.

***

Though the events happened a year ago the vivid memory stayed with Brian. He remembered how he dashed to the house to find police cars outside and a horde of neighbours all watching. It was true enough, Jan was dead and so was her father, Larry Stephens.

The post-mortem took place, but at the inquest, the blame implication was pure speculation - who was responsible for their deaths?

Naturally he gave a statement and gleaned all manner of information from the Detective Inspector Cliff Huxley in charge of the case. The DI showed Brian the bedroom where Jan had died and drew attention to the damaged windowpane. Something had scratched away the loose putty and broken the small pane of glass to enter the room.

Whatever it was, was small enough to have fitted through the opening: and it had also left the same way, since the front and the back doors were still secured on the inside when the police arrived. Brian found it puzzling, to say the least.

A young police constable found Jan dead with deep lacerations across her entire body, the blood drenching the white sheets. The face Brian knew and loved was contorted in death and carried horrific burn marks he couldn't explain away. Her hair had been flamed. Brian cried for her for many lonely months following her death. He loved her and the baby she was carrying.

From what the Inspector told Brian, Larry escaped to his study but had suffered the same fate as Jan. Even as he was talking to Brian on the phone the killer had broken down the door and got to him. Before he died, he'd drained half a bottle of whisky. As Brian knew Larry never touched the stuff, he guessed how scared he must have been. Death had been knocking on the door, yet Larry thought to warn him and the police. Brian knew he'd always miss him.

The inspector suggested a wild animal had got into the room, but it was so wild he could not put a name to it.

"To sum up, Dr Massey," the DI said, "we don't really know if we are on the right track. Some animal or thing did this killing. Let me assure you though, the police are concerned, we want to find the culprit before they kill again. Our Chief Superintendent has written a special report and is collating all information. I am sure we can solve this murder."

Brian remembered in his head the strange roar of the beast and the peculiar sound of flames as Larry was bitten and scorched to death. The animal was small, but could change its size, and spout flames. No animal he knew could do such a thing except the legendary dragon. Only something bizarre like that would have spooked Larry in such a way.

Since Jan and Larry died, Brian devoted much time in researching dragons and their customs, but still he's not an expert. Besides research, Brian remained vigilant on local incidents because he knew if a dormant dragon existed, it had to be in the Faringdon area.

After a while, his interest in odd occurrences made him wonder how quite a few people went missing late at night near Badbury Clump. Camera teams and reporters flocked to try and discover if something sinister lurked at the National Trust site. But after weeks of searching the police failed to uncover any clues. Brian made his own notes and drew apt conclusions.

Months later Brian remembered the death of Gloria Peppard, a farm worker, in her own cottage, again only a mile away from Faringdon. The Thames Valley Police found the dead woman with strange cuts about her face and burnt hair.

The next death gained a lot of coverage on the local Oxford Radio channel when a stranded woman motorist died in her car; again her body suffered from lacerations and burnt hair. The police issued many warnings but they seemed, to Brian, to be somewhat slow in their investigations. The concerned public followed the police progress as they looked for a killer. There seemed a marked reluctance by the police to declare a killer-dragon was at large. Brian speculated a decision might have been taken to dampen down reports in case it caused the general public to panic. Perhaps 'D' notices had been served to keep the situation under control. It reminded Brian of wartime when the Ministry of Defence clamped down on media coverage.

***

The months passed by relentlessly after Jan and Larry's deaths. Brian forced himself to take up new interests and hobbies in order to avoid dwelling on his loss. He increased his workload, which was fine up to a point. What he found of most benefit was meeting somebody who could understand his emotions. Brian found such a person in Valerie Morgan, an administrator who worked at the same Institute. His relationship with her started quite casually, when he remarked how he enjoyed going to the theatre in Oxford. From that single remark things developed between them for the good. Brian enjoyed it when Valerie invited him around for an evening meal.

***

At thirty-five Valerie was just two years younger than Brian. It was her soft grey eyes which attracted him in the first place; they were lovely and reflected her caring nature. In her face she showed a degree of sophistication, the way she dressed and her personal grooming, the thought she put into everything she did. Her sense of humour meant he loved being near her and keeping her company. And he was always reminded by the fullness of her lips, painted a delicate shade of pink, her slim body and welcoming arms.

Whenever he mentioned his thoughts or fears she never ever made light of them. Often she suggested things he'd never even thought about. He found her views so down to earth and stimulating they clarified his thoughts. He told her about his list of people who died in strange circumstances over the past year. It was on her advice he sent a copy of his findings in a note to the DI in charge of Jan's case. That was about two months earlier and he received an acknowledgement saying his letter would get due consideration and attention.

Because of his work Brian often spent a lot of time at the Institute. One night as he made the rounds he found a nurse and orderly searching a particular cell: the patient had simply disappeared. He joined in the search and they went through the cell: it was actually a full-sized flat with all manner of luxuries, but no Sangaku Taki. In searching, Brian found an open window in the bedroom, which overlooked the massive courtyard, and in a cupboard, a bullet. The window, the bullet and the missing patient started him thinking. He pocketed the bullet, determined to find out more.

As Brian stood there lost in his private thoughts and looking at the painting of the Temple of Kannon in Asakusa on the wall he felt the inmate at his elbow. Brian didn't know where Sangaku came from, as the door to the bedroom was closed. Sangaku smiled the same inscrutable smile often seen when martial arts experts face their enemy. The confident smile gave nothing away, but Brian was not deceived.

From Sangaku Taki's records, Brian knew him to be Japanese. At one time Sangaku had been a monk and then become mentally unstable for no apparent reason. After a long search his family decided to use the facilities offered by the Institute whilst they considered other options quoted by various UK consultants. Sangaku's family, though in Japan, paid the Institute well to look after him and to cater for his every need. Brian always wondered what had been the trigger to unbalance his patient's mind. Was the answer here in Oxfordshire?

Sangaku Taki was strange looking; he was very small even for a Japanese man, with fine black hair combed straight back with a centre parting. His arms bore some unusual tattoo marks hidden normally by his clothing. Brian studied those tattoos when he first met him but they never told him much. They certainly were not like the tattoo marks that belonged to the blood relatives of the Yakusa clan. Brian noticed Sangaku's sallow complexion was emphasised by his black piercing eyes. The face was not attractive, rather plump in fact, with a slit for a mouth and eyes that stared too much. At times Sangaku's eyes unsettled Brian. It came as no surprise to him others at the Institute shared his feeling about Sangaku.

As Sangaku Taki never spoke English, they didn't discover from him right then where he had been hiding. But Brian wondered enough to quiz his family and he guessed they related his probing questions. With the Internet and the large Japanese community in Swindon the Institute never had any problem treating Sangaku. Brian even knew a friendly translator. Naturally he realised his questions might have put Sangaku on his guard, but he needed to know.

Finally Sangaku admitted he had been meditating when Brian looked for him. Perhaps the possibility was there but Brian felt sure he'd have seen Sangaku if indeed he'd been in the flat. Proving Sangaku had been elsewhere was a daunting task.

***

With the discovery of the bullet, Brian turned to his new love, Valerie. He told her everything he found. As she listened to his concerns he felt things becoming so much clearer. Brian listened as she advised him to get expert help with the forensic aspect of the bullet. It was over two months or more since he'd contacted the police and though he'd got a reply to his letter nothing more happened. On her insistence not to be complacent he sought out a detective agency that took three weeks to give Brian his answer. They confirmed the bullet he found in Sangaku's flat was fired from Larry's gun. When he told Valerie, she was ecstatic and now he realised he had the sort of proof he needed to make the police listen. He phoned them and made an appointment to see the Inspector when he returned from a gun course at Leeds

Armoury. While Brian waited to see him he decided to take Valerie away for a short holiday. They went to Newquay and Porthcawl and a cluster of other interesting little places strung along the coastline.

It seemed strange but on one of the days whilst Brian enjoyed some leisure time with Valerie, something took place involving Sangaku. Apparently he had gone with fellow inmates on a day trip with four trained members of staff. The weather was fine and for a change, the driver had taken the special coach up to the car park at the White Horse at Uffington. All seemed well until the coach approached the road at the foot of White Horse Hill. It was then that Sangaku had gone berserk. He'd lost his temper and started attacking one of the staff. The others had forced him into a straight-jacket to keep him under control. Brian was intrigued to learn the attack had happened at Dragon Hill opposite the spot where St. George killed the legendary dragon. It started Brian thinking…

Immediately he told Valerie and she rubbed her hands together. Her eyes confirmed just what he'd been thinking. Now he could hardly wait for the appointment to see the DI about his suspicions concerning Sangaku. Brian had been through a year of torture and now it seemed something might get resolved. He even rang the police to check the time and date of the appointment, he simply couldn't help doing that.

***

Two days later Brian and Valerie walked out at night across the dimly lit courtyard of the Institute. When Brian paused he felt something skim through the air just above him. It hissed and a blast of hot air scorched his face and then Valerie cried out, beating the air with her hands as a black shape latched onto her body. The thing, Brian called it a thing, lunged at her and he heard a gurgle which stifled the last scream she made as she collapsed in his arms. It happened so quickly he didn't have time to defend her.

Valerie died in seconds. Brian tasted blood on his lips from where he bit them as he held her close. Her blood was all over him. Once more his thoughts skipped back in time to when Jan died. He re-lived those hours of agony. Now it had returned to him and he didn't want to suffer the anguish and pain again. He cried for mercy.

Then they were all around Brian - arms catching hold - leading him away gently to wait for the police. He had tears and blood on his face and a deep aching in his heart. He realised they would never believe him. Especially when a good lawyer could suggest the bullet from Larry's gun was planted by Brian in Sangaku's flat. Instantly he knew things looked bad.

How could he explain it away? Valerie had died in his arms; he was the nearest person to her so he had to be the one who killed her.

The men in the white coats, like the one Brian often wore, smiled a condescending smile he interpreted as saying 'psychiatrist turns killer'. Brian spotted the look a mile off and it worried him.

The police sirens bugled away and the ambulance lights flashed all around Brian in the courtyard. He looked once more where Valerie lay covered by a blanket. And then amidst the entire bustle he heard the window slam shut high above his head. Instinctively he looked up knowing in a fraction of a second the dragon man was home.

Desert Dance

"There is a killer loose in the desert," Jarge Benson said, sixty years of loving the outdoor life in his weathered face and observant blue eyes, his black hair shot with grey.

"I read in the *Navajo Times*, that the Mafia guys Nazario Maldini and Elmo Nesta died while tied up with their elbows behind their back, their wrists lashed together in front and their ankles on a short piece of rope. Death Dance, the paper called it because they shuffled around their 4x4 until they died. There's speculation that they were looking for gold because of the many holes they'd dug in the desert. Already the Navajo Trickster Spirit is blamed because forensics found spider hairs on their bodies."

His companion was Fay Armstrong — a dark-haired, slightly overweight fifty-five-year-old lecturer from Detroit University — whose upturned nose hinted at plastic surgery, although there was nothing false about her.

"It's strange," she said. "But so is the number of Navajos who've died in their own hospitals, all struck down by an unidentified illness. It's spooky."

Jarge picked up the wine bottle and poured out two glasses of Spanish wine. He handed one to Fay.

The Navajo's five-star Anasazi Hotel in Four Corners, New Mexico, offered a breathtaking view of the desert from their room on the 7th floor, and enjoyed a good deal of tourist trade. This was the second time Jarge and Fay had visited the area and stayed there.

She dropped her files onto the table while Jarge took out his notes and opened his folders.

When Fay Armstrong knew Jarge planned to visit America it gave her the opportunity to book the hotel and renew their long-standing friendship of over ten years. She first met him and welcomed the support he offered when her husband died of cancer three years ago. With a chance to show Jarge some more American landscapes she obtained permits and engaged a guide for the LeChee district.

So far they'd visited the Navajo reservation, Antelope Canyon and an incredible waterfall. They watched Navajo women weaving baskets. On a craft stall Fay noticed many straw items. On an impulse she bought a hat, a spider and a doll. She also purchased a silver cross inlaid with tiny pieces of turquoise stone.

But throughout their sightseeing tour they heard the Navajo Nation Radio voice the thoughts of local tribal leaders about the dead Navajos and the Death Dance.

"I'll talk to the hotel manager," Jarge said. "He's Navajo and might have an angle on it all. Right, now let's finish this work and then we can go to dinner. OK."

***

Mafia man Nico Baggio lost control of his vehicle as his mind kept returning to the Death Dance performed by Nazario and Elmo. Now he had to locate the drugs they failed to find. As the 4x4 hit a rock at speed it veered off the official road and landed in softer sand. The engine grated, then stopped as it overheated.

Nico glanced at the empty water container and reached for the whisky bottle. He wiped his mouth on the sleeve of his shirt. Sweating in the unbearable heat, he was also aware 'something' out there spooked him. He sat in the vehicle his eyes fixed on the desert road he'd left.

After a few minutes he used his cell phone to leave a call for help on an answering machine. He prepared himself for the long wait. Then he gasped at what came over the skyline...

***

"Trickster Spirit can change into anything, any animal," the hotel manager Martin Yazzie said. "Sure Nazario and Elmo died. I'm modern Navajo with a degree from East Tennessee State University. Still parts of me wonder about the old myths; it's my heritage.

"The Death Dance is for condemned prisoners. Now that's what gets to me. A bad spirit? I'm inclined to think it's out there in the desert."

A bead of sweat appeared on Jarge's forehead in spite of the air conditioning.

"In England we have malevolent spirits, so maybe America is no different. Now do you really believe in the old way? And Trickster?"

Martin Yazzie smiled. "Yes. Some things change but old fears always linger."

"OK but I'm curious," Fay said. "You've heard more than gossip?"

"Perhaps. I'm guessing at the Trickster because of the spider hairs on the dead Mafia men." Martin looked at the silver cross around Fay's neck, then at the straw items she'd bought recently. "I like your choice. That's an excellent cross and you are helping us Navajos." He picked up the straw spider and placed it on a glass table. Jarge and Fay watched in amazement as the legs of the straw spider jerked slightly and it appeared to walk across the tabletop. "Is it static or is the Trickster making that happen? I'll let you decide," Martin said.

***

"Heck, speculation is running rife," Martin said ten days later. "I've even heard some mystics claim Trickster is back as a spider, a coyote, even a woman." Martin said. "Our shaman stay with the old rituals but many have turned to witchcraft and black magic. But all agree 'something' is in the air. I saw a reference to it in the *Navajo Times*. They reported it as Bad Medicine; the thing the elders find so saddening in the young today."

"Holy Toledo. You're not kidding. That is some strong stuff you are coming out with," Jarge said.

"Yep. Trickster frightens me too," Martin said with a smile. "An evil spirit that can change into any form, can certainly scare. No doubt about that."

"Oh yes, the spider, the coyote and the woman?" Jarge said. "I sort of remember some juju stuff from Rhodesia. It was to do with unwelcome animals and things. The local medicine man used fire to find the person using black magic. It worked. Fire was the key. I need to remember more details. There was also something about holding a burning piece of coal. If you were guilty you dropped it. Who knows what might help here?"

Fay laughed and drank some wine.

"Animals. Juju. Trickster. Who knows for sure? Now you sound spooky. And you mention a woman too. Funny how women and Trickster get lumped together. But that's men for you," Fay said. She laughed.

***

The next morning a police car sped down the road past the hotel. It moved quickly, kicking up clouds of dust whilst its sirens announced the urgency. When there was silence again Jarge and Fay wondered if there'd been another killing. Then an ambulance sped down the road in the wake of the police car.

At breakfast Jarge spoke to the manager again. "Tell me, Martin," Jarge said, "I thought about what you said. Forget the Death Dance thing but are the Navajos cursed or what? I'm talking about those dead Navajos in hospital."

"I take your point," Martin returned, "others think the same. Mystics have linked all the deaths with a strange sound. People seem to die when that sound is heard. One person likened the noise to wind blowing through Window Rock Mountain."

"A strange sound?"

Fay looked at Martin and Jarge. "The wind through the hole creates weird effects," she said.

Martin nodded. "Perhaps. I know I've heard the wind carry a strange sound over the desert some nights. I told the elders. One thing though, us Navajos in the know are carrying this for protection." Martin showed them a tiny straw dolly. "Might be best if you carried one too."

Fay didn't answer but fingered the silver cross around her neck. They all stared out through the window at the desert when they heard a strange sound...

***

"The police have got a man," Martin Yazzie said. He gave them the news two days later. "This guy Ottavia Cannavaro was caught red-handed with a huge haul of drugs. Plus the guy has made a statement implicating the other three dead Mafia men. Ottavia kept firing his gun and seemed really scared when the police arrested him. He claimed 'something' was coming out of the desert at him. He was glad the police turned up."

Jarge smiled wryly. "At least he didn't have to dance his way to death like the other Mafia guys did. Is that the end of it all?"

"Maybe but there is still that sound," Martin replied. "I don't mean to worry but I'm not well. Even with the straw dolly to help I need backup from the medicine man. Let's hope the old rituals succeed."

Fay looked at Martin Yazzie and read his expression. "My God. We're sorry to hear that. Now the Mafia man has been caught and the drugs found, surely the spirit has finished its work? We still hope you get well quickly." She started to fidget with the silver cross around her neck.

"A bad or malevolent spirit keeps doing evil," Jarge said. "I remember in England a corn gathering ceremony in the autumn. It's to do with checking the evil spirit of the earth. Navajo's ways are much the same as in other parts of the world. In Rhodesia, I mentioned earlier about fire and animals. The two don't mix, as fire is a cleanser if used correctly. Often suggestion can play havoc with what we think. If Navajo think they will get ill and die, then it might happen. Everything is all in the mind. I guess. Even the spirit Trickster. Fay, I fancy a break, so where shall we go to do more sightseeing?"

"Fine. Perhaps the Butterfly Canyon might be a good place to check out. I never get tired of seeing the place. Be a good fellow and book up a guide for us and while you do that I'll sort out any permits we might need."

Later on that day Jarge drove out towards Butterfly Canyon to meet the guide assigned to them. Jarge watched the desert on both sides of the car as he drove. He saw something, slowed down and reversed for another look.

"What's up?" Fay asked.

"Not quite sure but I've got to look."

Once out of the car Jarge led the way to the spot that caught his attention. They stared at the three sticks pushed into the sand and tied together with narrow strips of coloured material. A small figure woven in corn hung down from the point where the three sticks were tied together. Jarge picked up the doll.

"What is it?" Fay asked. She slid her sunglasses back to the top of her head and took a photograph.

"A clue I guess," Jarge said. "It's like the dolly Martin showed us, the one that keeps him alive. I think I'll hang on to this one for my own protection. So we should both be safe as now we've each got a dolly." Jarge paused and held up his hand to make Fay listen. "That sound? Hear it?"

Fay nodded. The whispering sound carried right across the desert on a light breeze. It touched a spot inside her mind and made her shiver. They returned to the car and as they continued the journey they talked about the corn dolly.

***

Jarge and Fay showed the permits to the guide Johnny Sestawale at the trailhead.

"Thanks, I'm sure glad of the work," Johnny said. "In only one hour I'll make you love Butterfly Canyon."

When the visit ended an hour later they were excited with all they'd seen and moved to another destination.

Fay yearned to look at more Navajo rugs, especially the well-known Crystal design and the Two Grey Hills. Together they studied the rugs at the craft stall near the Butterfly Canyon and Jarge made a present of one to Fay.

Their return to the hotel brought unwelcome news; Martin Yazzie had gone home after falling sick. He now awaited a visit from the medicine man.

They also spread out the Navajo rug on the floor and walked on it, feeling the texture. But as they did that they couldn't help but think what might lie out there in the desert.

***

Late at night the phone rang in their hotel room. Jarge picked it up as Fay sat on the edge of the bed brushing her hair. Jarge heard Martin Yazzie speak.

"What's wrong?" Jarge said. "I thought you were sick."

"True. I was," Martin said. "But our medicine man treated me. He also says there is a stubborn spirit out there. The spirit is clever, like Trickster.

"He used my straw doll in a ritual. And it worked too."

Jarge picked up the straw doll he'd found in the desert and described it to Martin.

"Yes, that's it. Keep it with you," Martin said. "For your good luck."

Jarge gave Fay a quick push with his hand to get her attention.

"Maybe it's too late for that," Jarge said He heard an unusual noise on the balcony. He dropped the phone on the bed; watched the curtain blow in the breeze. Fay looked at him her eyes wide open in apprehension. He frowned and strained his eyes to glimpse what lay in the shadows. He sweated, hardly daring to breathe.

He kept watch; heard a shrill sound come from out of the desert. The sound made him shiver as Fay drew closer to him and the curtains moved slightly.

In the light breeze Jarge caught the heady whiff of perfume, so unlike the expensive Chanel Fay wore. The perfume filled the whole room with its cloying fragrance. Jarge swallowed hard.

In one hand he held the straw doll and then he felt something pressed into his other hand. He looked down; saw the silver cross Fay had removed from around her neck. Jarge wrapped the silver cross around the straw doll and then glanced back at the curtain.

As it parted slightly, a dark shape emerged. Jarge stared at it in horror, remembering Martin's warning. He stood in front of Fay and prepared to face what lay ahead.

Nothing happened for a few minutes. The shape he'd seen seemed to have gone but Jarge was suspicious. He waited a long minute and then prepared himself for confrontation. Carefully he advanced towards the curtain. He lifted the curtain edge and pulled it aside. He gasped as he stopped. Then in front of Jarge the shadowy shape reared up to greet him. He heard Fay scream.

The shape shimmered, as it became recognizable. Jarge saw the trim figure of a woman, flowing black hair, rich red lips, and eyes that blazed like yellow fires. The woman shot out a hand to catch Jarge. Immediately Jarge set fire to the straw dolly with a cigarette lighter. As the straw burnt, Jarge thrust it into the woman's open hand. It was a fire trick he'd learnt in Rhodesia. He hoped it would work.

The violent reaction caught Jarge by surprise. The woman screamed with pain as the flames burnt and she seemed unable to escape from the burning doll.

They watched the woman jerk violently as she ran around the balcony in agony, her tormented cry filling the night. Then as the screaming reached a crescendo, the woman leapt over the wall of the balcony.

It was too dark for them to determine where the evil thing had gone. As they watched they saw a moving pinprick of light heading off into the desert. The desert Dance of Death. That was it. At short intervals they heard the cry until at long last it stopped. Somewhere out there they might find the cross but Jarge wondered if they should even bother looking. Now they'd got rid of the desert spirit, the Trickster, they certainly didn't want contact with it again.

Jarge phoned Martin Yazzie and let him know what happened. After the call Jarge removed a bottle of champagne from the fridge. He poured out two glasses and gave one to Fay. With all the excitement Jarge noticed how her eyes stayed so wide open and shining. She looked more beautiful than the evil spirit. They sipped the champagne and Jarge decided this was the best spirit of the desert he knew. The other Trickster spirit belonged to the past.

"Gosh Van Gogh"

Cornelius Rothchild, the celebrated expert on war games, faced a hall full of specially invited people. The security guards at the rear monitored anybody entering or leaving and they controlled the doors.

"I loved the Roman *ballista,* so good in its day. My company 2030 Inc. is also brilliant, but look around and see for yourself. First I've laid on a short demo for us all before I break some stupendous news."

Immediately the audience buzzed at his words, their eyes on the gelatine block set in tough plastic on the table before them. They watched as army experts prepared the equipment for a ballistics demonstration.

He pressed a red button on a control panel to send some fifty tiny arrows into the gelatine block. The audience clapped with delight as they awaited the results of the trial.

The huge smile Cornelius wore told the whole story.

"In this mock battle, twenty Flemish bowmen have outclassed thirty Burgandian bowmen. It's a remarkable result and might explain why I adore war games.

"But the burning issue today concerns achievable Time Travel."

Next came the dramatic pause followed by gasps of disbelief. Throughout the hall the audience buzzed with excitement as they discussed the possibility of Time Travel. Only the MD of 2030 knew how to promote his company in such a way. It was obvious from the manner in which they watched Cornelius that they all wanted to know more.

The reporter Nicole Garfield wrote furiously in her notebook. She tossed her hair with excitement and clutched at the sleeve of her colleague.

"I knew it," Nicole whispered intently. "Time Travel is what it's all about. Tell me I'm dreaming this, but I can see megabucks here. Hell! I'm ecstatic, as I know our *Hello* readers will want to know about this latest technical thing. I, for one, want to know the truth behind

Marilyn Monroe. Maybe with Time Travel we can cash in on this interest for the past. Who knows? I guess it sounds too good to be true."

The gasps and the buzz continued. At the back of the hall a cluster of reporters from *Jane's Defence* made their notes. They watched the screens and the overhead projectors as Cornelius continued with his talk. The reporters made military weapons their lifeblood and if what they heard became fact, they already guessed at the implications plus the money involved.

"Imagine it," the senior reporter from JD told his colleagues, "we could move a thousand men to anywhere in the world in one second. Listen to what he says and then I'll talk to you after. Heck, I'm so excited I don't want to miss a trick."

After half an hour of listening to the talk, a government minister from China covered the pad on his lap with elaborate notes. Already the excitement welled up within him when he thought of all the possibilities Time Travel could mean to the Chinese nation. The mind-blowing technology might solve spent uranium disposal problems and even help with discovering new life-saving drugs from the future.

Cornelius held up his hand, then pointed at a suit of armour on a stand.

"We've captured the military uniform of General Julius Caesar." Once more the audience gasped. They looked at one another and leaned forward. "It really is a work of art, as verified by our art experts here today. On the slides you've seen how the uniform got here. But I've more surprises in store when I hand you over to Paul."

A fair-haired man of about thirty-five years old stepped onto the stage and took over the microphone. He indicated the pictures appearing on the large screen in the hall and explained what he had in mind.

"Hi, I'm Paul Henderson and work for 2030 Inc. I'm interested in all paintings by Van Gogh. I've traced all of them but by chance I've found one exists that people have overlooked. Everybody knows about the girlfriend. What I hope to do is to travel back in time and get hold of the painting by Van Gogh featuring his severed ear.

"I'm wearing everything I need to travel through time; ISSOchips have made this possible so there is no heavy machine for me to sit on. All I need for control is strapped around my belt." Paul looked across at Cornelius and then the audience. "I've been given the signal everything is set. Right let's go for it! *Geronimo*!"

Cornelius pressed a switch to make Paul disappear in a spectacular blue light. The audience sat there spellbound. Then they started asking questions.

From the nature of the experiment and seeing it happen before them no magical trick was involved. Many of the audience left their seats to come to the front of the stage to tap the floor where Paul had stood. They examined it as if half expecting a trapdoor to open.

Cornelius watched them with good humour. He answered many of their questions and time passed quickly. Then ten minutes later the lights dimmed and the power surge influenced electrical equipment in the hall.

As the power cut took place, his forehead creased as his worry showed from the way he screwed up his mouth. Clearly the disruption was causing him problems. Cornelius used his phone to call for technical help and seemed relieved when an electrician appeared and started to check the equipment.

Once the electrician declared everything safe, the massive speakers alongside the stage burst into life. First came the loud crackling followed by Paul's voice.

"Hello, hello. I can't hear you. My two-way radio is playing up. Hope you can hear. We've had a loss of power or something. But it seems to have been fixed. Cornelius, I've found Van Gogh. At the moment he's mixing up paints. He's strange; keeps looking at me. He's mad! A real nutcase! As soon as I've got the painting off him I'll be on my way back."

The message came to a halt and nothing happened for the next half-hour. Then without warning Paul appeared slumped in a wooden chair. His eyes stayed shut. From the way he screwed up his face and moaned he looked to be in great pain. The audience shot to their feet, some surged forward for a better view. Those nearest noticed how Paul held in his right hand a painting of a severed ear.

"Oh! My God," Cornelius shouted. "He's hurt. Somebody get a doctor. Call an ambulance."

Paul held the painting in one hand whilst trying to stem the flow of blood with his other hand. The audience saw the cloth covered in blood where he pressed it against the side of his head. The acute pain distorted his features making it impossible for him to talk. A doctor appeared and immediately started to administer First Aid. The audience watched in silence, and then ten minutes later they heard the sound of an ambulance racing to the scene with full sirens blaring.

The audience gasped.

"But it's his ear!" Cornelius shouted and echoed all their thoughts.

An art expert at the front of the hall realised the implication and pointed at the painting with trembling fingers. "I'd know that signature and style anywhere. This is a Van Gogh painting. It's for real."

The sinister implications hit hard even though the audience had been primed to expect the painting and to see time travel being demonstrated. It might have been too surreal for them to take in all at once. The audience gasped.

The same art expert touched the canvas lightly with his fingers. The expression on his face changed, forcing the audience to read the meaning on his face.

In minutes they witnessed Paul's severed ear and the discovery of a new Van Gogh painting. Both incidents shocked them.

But what truly shocked them, was the realisation that the paint on the Van Gogh canvas was so wet. As wet as the blood on Paul's neck.

Dragon Skin

I'm so scared, so frightened of meeting myself on today of all days, Friday the thirteenth. Superstitious? An odd phobia? Perhaps. But listen...

I guess I've never been lucky with numbers: thirteen is my worst one. And the date Friday the thirteenth always reminds me when bad things often happen.

I can remember when our house burnt down; my parents' death in a car crash and how I nearly died assisting a drowning man. All those traumatic events took place on Friday the thirteenth.

When I saved the life of a Hare Krishna priest I was, at the time, a soldier in the Foreign Legion in Orange, France. It was pure chance I was on the riverbank when I saw him struggling in the water. His plight was desperate, so in seconds I jumped in to save him. I was a good swimmer and though the current was strong I managed to get him back on dry land.

A full five minutes passed before he even recovered enough to talk. He explained how, as a senior Hare Krishna priest, he was travelling to a temple in Bombay to hand over a sacred relic. I watched in fascination as he took out a slim packet wrapped in polythene from his ochre robes. Soon he held up what looked like a piece of green parchment but it was covered with strange scales. I was intrigued and asked him what it was and why was it so special. First he asked my name and then his reply sent a shiver down my spine.

"Dragon skin. This is ancient dragon's skin, Angus; I must deliver it to the Pratnava Temple in Bombay. The skin is from the famous thirteenth dragon of this same temple. It was sent to America for a special ritual to bring peace in these ever troubled times, and must go back to its shrine.

"The thirteenth dragon is a creature of God and all God's creatures have a need for love. The thirteenth dragon's skin represents many magical and healing powers.

"Our temple is devoted to achieving peace in the future through the use of this sacred relic. All bad things must be forgotten as we face exciting times. But there are some people who will make money out of the poor, the scourge of famine and the start of any war. These people have been on my trail for a long time. They are desperate to get their hands on this thirteenth dragon's skin to perform their own vile form of black magic."

The priest took the thirteenth dragon's skin to touch my forehead with it as he chanted strange words. I felt a pulsating chain reaction as an electric shock raced through my body. It left me tingling as if a mountain stream was running through my veins. I was full of excitement.

The Hare Krishna priest continued.

"Because of your kind act in saving me and the thirteenth dragon's skin, I have given you the protection only offered to a few people. One day I will make a point of repaying you for saving my life. I promise you.

"I seem to have lost one of my sandals, Angus. Please check I didn't drop it by the river bank."

I went to look and on my return there was no sign of the Hare Krishna priest.

***

Those events were years ago. Today, things came to a head at the Underground station. I glanced at a man on the other commuter train. He resembled me in so many ways. The beard, the tie, the suit, even the *Guardian* newspaper he carried, all added to the illusion of something common between us but yet so bizarre. And today was only the third…

"Strange thing, on the train this morning, Charlotte."

My wife widened her green eyes and looked at me. She was beautiful but could be touchy at times. She tossed her red hair in exasperation.

"Hell! Angus. Twelve million people here in London, of course one might look like you. As a computer wizard you ought to know the odds."

I resolved to say no more: I went and watched Paula, our nine-year-old, play on her piano. She loved music because it made her so happy.

The next day I dressed in my special green suit with shirt and tie to match. I carried a raincoat over my arm. I got on my usual train and waited.

Yes. He was there dressed exactly like me. But it was different seeing him for the second time: I stared at his face and saw my own face looking back. I shuddered. Was it all a coincidence?

All the time I was at work I kept wondering about the man, only too aware I'd lost a certain edge. Who was he? Was he some kind of alien being? Nothing was making any sense. I shook my head, wondering if reading too much science fiction was to blame.

As I ate breakfast on the fifth, Charlotte appraised my clean-shaven face and kissed my cheek. She smiled and one eyebrow lifted. When I saw that eyebrow go up I thought I'd lost my slim 12 stone image because of her discerning look. "No beard? I don't mind: it makes you look younger, Angus. But are you going to work like that?"

"Sure. I've got a game of squash first thing so I've already changed to save time."

I was amazed when he appeared on the other train because his beard was gone too and he wore the same blue and white shell suit I wore. It also carried the legend 'East Texas State University.'

That to me felt like a body blow and it became my constant worry. Everybody noticed my mood: Charlotte said so quite bluntly. I took her advice and saw my doctor who said I was clearly under stress. He suggested taking a holiday, a break. It prompted me to book a few days in the country town of Faringdon. A holiday sounded better than tablets anytime.

On the following Saturday we travelled down by car to the rented cottage. On our first evening we had a barbecue: it was great. During the rest of our stay we enjoyed ourselves walking, looking at the Tithe barn at Great Coxwell and visiting the haunted old Mill at Thrupp.

We even visited the famous battlefield at White Horse Hill, Uffington. I remember sitting on a grassy slope looking down many hundreds of feet to a black ribbon of a road and the place, the other side of the road, where St. George killed the dragon.

I found my thoughts returned to that Hare Krishna priest. It was strange I had not thought of him for years. I wondered if he managed to get to the Pratnava temple in Bombay with the green skin of the thirteenth dragon. I hoped his mission was successful.

Paula loved the country experience and she even took part in the local Folly Fun Run around the famous 140-ft tower. I enjoyed the great unwinding, visiting the many old pubs and drinking the real ale. We visited a Red Dragon pub in Coxwell Street, where I met an old timer. I bought him a pint of 'Speckled Hen' and we chatted for over an hour. The old man certainly knew a lot about dragon folklore.

The days sped by and we returned to London on the twelfth night. On the Friday morning I was a new man: my cheeks were full of colour and I gained such energy. The air, the countryside, my family, all worked wonders for my health.

Today, Friday the thirteenth, I got up early to wash and shave with great care. I picked out a good quality grey suit, the tie was my Birtley College one from university days. I splashed on the Eau Savage, fixed a red flower in my buttonhole and went downstairs. It was time for work.

I wanted my mind clear of disturbing thoughts: but even the feeling of well-being after a holiday has to contend with the thirteenth bug. And to cap it all today was also a Friday...

Seconds ticked by, making me restless. Again I checked my watch. LATE! My train was late. Thirty seconds more was all I was going to give it. Thirty seconds later I lost control. I must see him: to confront him. For my sanity I knew I must!

I ran up and down the stairs crossing on to the far platform as the other train pulled in. I jumped on board and searched for him: I was determined to find him.

But I didn't: instead, on his usual seat lay the *Guardian* which we both read. I snatched it up.

Moments later the train started with me on board and going in the wrong direction. As it did, I saw the man. He too was dressed like me, even down to the red buttonhole and Birtley tie. It shook me. I couldn't explain what was happening.

But in fractions of a second we made eye contact: I detected nothing evil there. Even as I watched, his face smiled, a generous smile, and an imp discernible in that smile, a devil-may-care look. He was like a debonair Simon Templar, especially with that halo glowing around his head. Did I read him right? He waved: I waved. It was sheer upmanship! I was sweating: he was sweating. I pulled a hanky from my pocket to wipe my forehead and as the train drew away I caught a glimpse of something ochre in his hand.

A loud explosion followed minutes later; the train stopped, the lights went out. Girls screamed, men lit matches and voices appealed for calm. I never found time to think. All around, workmen moved along the track. We were in darkness and anything could happen.

It did: another bomb exploded some distance away but we all felt the shock waves. And we could do nothing. Eventually we got back to the station an hour later: in that period the sirens wailed the warning and flashing lights told of a major train disaster. A lot of people died on that other train.

I admit I was puzzled by the sequence of events. I recollected the ochre cloth the man had in his hand. It stirred other thoughts within me. The priest I'd saved all those years back. I struggled to put it in perspective. Maybe this was his way of repaying his debt to me. He did say he would. It had been so long ago I'd forgotten all about it.

The number of emergency staff there at the station indicated the seriousness of the situation. My heart beat faster when I saw them: Charlotte and Paula looked so worried. They stood there in the crowd, crying. But I was lucky I wasn't on the wrecked train. I felt good. I shouted. I loved them. I was alive!

"Oh Dad! Oh Dad! I love you."

Paula kept crying.

"Dad, we were so worried, we thought…we thought…they said there were no survivors…it was on the telly."

Paula blew her nose in a hanky. She wiped her eyes.

I didn't know what to say so I hugged her tight and led the way to the exit from the station.

"You were lucky, Angus, not being on your usual train," Charlotte whispered in my ear, her voice husky with emotion. She squeezed my hand as I led the way outside into the fresh air. I was in the middle holding Paula and Charlotte close to me: people looked at our tear-streaked faces and let us pass.

To my surprise, as if from nowhere, I saw the shaven heads of six young Hare Krishna men: they carried musical instruments and were dressed in their familiar ochre robes. I slipped a banknote to Paula: she dropped it in their wooden bowl. I always liked to help the underdog: I'd been there in the Legion myself and knew how tough life could be. They also reminded me of someone I once met…The priest…

"So why did you swap trains?" Charlotte asked. She looked pale with dark rings under her eyes. They were still moist from crying. Her make-up was smudged and her hair windswept.

"I still don't know how to answer your question. It's as if

something told me to change trains. I can't explain the feeling. I felt it was the right thing to do. Like some being was looking after me."

***

Later back at home I enjoyed a cup of coffee. It was still Friday and the thirteenth but I was alive. If I'd caught the 'other' train...

I guessed at the esoteric, the cosmic world: things I often couldn't fathom. I tried to find the right words to express my feelings but it was so difficult. A sense of *déjà vu* flooded over me. What was it made me miss my train? And who was the man with the halo around his head? A saint? A guardian angel? An Angel of the Lord? Perhaps.

Images tumbled into my mind's eye of those young men who chanted as they circled to hang garlands around our necks.

"HARE KRISHNA! HARE KRISHNA! HARE KRISHNA! HARE! HARE!"

Paula had been so thrilled at the attention. She loved the music. I knew from the way her eyes sparkled: she was radiant.

I decided to ask her a question.

"Tell me, Paula, what did the Krishna boys sing?"

"Dad, it was so easy 'cause you know I love music, even foreign music. Here listen, I'll sing it for you."

From the way Paula spoke I knew she was already over her initial shock.

As my sweet daughter started to sing the pulsating almost hypnotic chant, Charlotte looked deep into my eyes as she squeezed my hand. I knew she was seeing a certain look on my face of far-away places, of bad days in the Legion, of a debt repaid...

***

So you see, things always catch up with me on Friday the thirteenth. I caught a wrong train, I nearly got killed, and the Hare Krishna boys sang a tune which keeps haunting me for some unknown reason. I also love the way my Paula chanted their song even though she doesn't know what the words mean. I find life is so full of mystery, particularly today.

By chance I remembered the newspaper and laid it on the kitchen table. A photo on the front page leapt out at me showing Charlotte,

Paula and me in the middle surrounded by devotees of the Hare Krishna sect. I noted the garland of flowers around our necks.

"Guardian Angel Saved Angus", declared the bold headlines. Maybe that was it.

I gasped at the surreal story carried in the newspaper I held which, betrayed by the date, I knew hadn't even rolled off tomorrow's printing presses.

Silver Wolf

The constant jangle of the horses' harness didn't frighten me but the sudden sound of silence did; it meant death for somebody.

For two days I, Mikhail Razumovsky, stayed with Anna, my wife, confined to our cottage, waiting for the Ninth Kazanski Cossacks to finish their search. Each day the Russian horsemen searched the woods and open countryside around our cottage for the two escaped murderers. At night-time huge fires burned as our soldiers kept watch in case the desperate men tried to slip out of the cordon thrown around the area.

Eventually I heard the brief gunshots. It signalled to me the execution of the cornered men. The Cossacks dug the graves in the local churchyard, they buried the men and left. I couldn't wait for Boris, my brother-in-law to return from the army camp to tell us his tall Cossack tales, invented over a bottle of vodka.

***

"The silver wolf! It's the devil, I swear it is. Mikhail, don't go, I beg you."

I kissed my dear, but elderly, wife. She worried so much. But I remember ever since our marriage how she always showed concern for me.

I, Mikhail, was always easy going, but then at sixty a man depends on his creature comforts. Anna cooked well enough to make me overweight with a round face. I often joked I'd no grey hairs but that was because I was bald. I've also spat out a few teeth over the years and laughed that I never wanted them. I'm an old Russian with a limp and, like Boris, I rely on vodka to keep me going.

"Anna, we need firewood for our stove. I must find more wood to burn. And the wolf myth! Some peasant saw it a hundred years ago.

Boris says he saw the silver wolf but he is so mad, so old and always so full of vodka. I blame you, Anna, for him getting drunk; I think it must be something to do with him being your brother. I don't mind, Boris has a kind heart and a thirst for good vodka. But look, I'll be fine. So don't worry. If I don't get back in time for supper, call Boris and he'll tell his Cossack friends," I joked. "They always help against ghosts or even the silver wolf."

I made my way to the graveyard looking for the two new graves. I gazed at the wooden crosses pushed into the soil, pausing slightly before lifting them out.

An hour later my sack felt like lead though I'd only filled it with stolen wooden crosses. I learnt a lot about survival, while living in the bleak Russian countryside. My short time in Moscow also taught me how to look in the right places for fuel. Ever since my injury two years ago I didn't work. But my injury didn't stop me from gathering wooden crosses to burn on our stove. In the summer I made and sold crosses, so it worked out well for me.

When I dragged the sack behind me it dug into the ground; pulling it past the headstones of Russian heroes began to exhaust me. My aching knee didn't help either.

No official person tended the graves or dug new ones, not since Zacho the Russian Armenian dwarf disappeared.

I remembered the dwarf; his head sported thick short black hair, his deep chest shaped like a barrel. Sometimes he grew a beard but always he wore his tunic tied around the middle with a piece of rope. Besides his evident deafness, Zacho never spoke. How he managed to survive puzzled me; but he did somehow. His gypsy background maybe helped a little but I felt it upset his attitude to life.

Zacho claimed grave digging as his own niche: if a person died, he'd dig the grave instantly. If several persons died, he'd soon have the graves dug out to please the clergyman and the relatives. On one occasion he dug an extra grave. It generated excitement in the village with guesses as to who would fill the vacant plot.

One day Zacho disappeared. His whereabouts was a mystery to the locals. But always people died and graves needed to be dug. It compelled relatives to dig graves when their loved ones died. I cast a glance back at the newest graves. It was easy to see how the Cossacks put their mark on the graves with military preciseness. They always dug good graves.

After Zacho's disappearance, it was Boris who spotted the

gravedigger on a single occasion many months later. One meeting seemed enough. Good old Boris talked though his vodka stupor about seeing the dwarf studying each grave. To Boris it seemed as if something mattered to Zacho. Perhaps it did, but checking out graves late at night was certainly open to much speculation.

***

When I glanced at the grey skies I noticed the snow clouds. The keen, sabre-toothed Siberian wind cut creases into my face. Quickly I drew my coat tighter around me and drank some vodka to keep warm.

The lingering, drawn-out howl of a wolf shattered the silence. I hated the sound, which to me, signalled evil. I looked around, but where could I go to avoid being caught in the open? The wolf howl sounded again. Closer. My breathing quickened, sweat broke out on my face and hands. A normal reaction in such a situation, I guessed.

The bestial howling seemed to emerge from the depth of Hades. In listening to it I felt it chill my blood. The wolf hunted. Hunted. Me, Mikhail, I was sure. My gut instincts never let me down.

My gaze swept the land sprinkled with snow that sloped away from the graveyard. I looked beyond the fields and watched how the snow swirled, blown by the wind. I searched, trying to detect a movement. I looked far away in the direction where I expected to see the wolf. Then something moved. A second later I saw that flash of silver zipping through the trees. The wolf. It existed. Boris was right - the silver wolf was here. I, Mikhail Razumovsky, felt scared as it headed my way. And towards the graveyard. Soon only a low stone wall separated me from the creature. Such a mild barrier poised no threat to the wolf that made myths linger and frighten. Closer. A snarl replaced the howling. It was deep, throaty and increased with evident ferocity as the silver wolf launched itself through the air.

I panicked as the wolf leaped. I half expected it to land this side of the wall but it didn't. Instead it landed on something crouched under the wall. I could imagine the scene. I heard the sound as a woman screamed in terror. Next came the wolf attack as it tore into her flesh. Then the last scream cut off abruptly. Now the woman was a victim to the hungry wolf.

I never guessed a woman was so close to the graveyard. I wondered who she was. Even if I didn't know her name I made the sign of the cross and immediately moved myself as I looked for protection. Now she had died at the hands of the wolf and the worry made me suffer a bout of conscience. I, scared Mikhail Razumovsky, who'd done nothing to help.

***

The weather changed in minutes; heavy snow driven by biting winds fell, driving the wolf out into the wilds as it looked for shelter. But I knew it would be back.

In desperation to escape from the storm, I broke into a large mausoleum. Quickly and carefully I removed the wooden cover on the one I selected to climb inside, bags and all, securing the entrance with a piece of string.

I sat in darkness protected from the wind, wondering about the snow and the wolf outside. I gathered some leaves and lit a fire for warmth and light. I rested as the storm outside developed an unusual intensity. I peeped out but could see nothing, with the blizzard blanketing everything. It was so quiet under the thick layers of snow. I tried to sleep but woke up at about midnight, my head full of weird dreams involving satanic cults, rituals involving the wolf that howled in the night.

At first light, I pushed the wooden hatch open to witness a graveyard smothered by deep snow. I closed the wooden cover and wondered what to do. The coldness prompted me to start a fresh fire. As I gathered up the thick bed of dry leaves I realised I had taken them off the face of a dead man. I dug deep to find the rest of his body. I remained in shock knowing he'd been lying there all the time with me in the dark. I shivered. I hadn't even noticed him. Now I trembled. I wish it had been because of the cold.

The surreal situation continued as if I'd been drinking too much vodka like Boris; it was a feeling I couldn't shake off, after those strange dreams of mine. I sniffed. It was true. I could smell rich, succulent food cooking somewhere close by. Images tumbled through my head, screams from a different level of memory echoed through my head. I heard. This was too surreal, too scary for me, Mikhail Razumovsky, a poor Russian trying to find fuel for a home fire.

The wobbly yellow light that came towards me from the deep recesses of the stone chamber seemed too surreal. As the light drew closer it threw strange shapes and shadows across the walls.

Next I heard a simple noise; a foot dragged along, followed by the sound like that of a knife scraped on a stone wall. I swallowed hard, wondering whether to run or stay.

While I debated what to do, the cover of the mausoleum flew open. Immediately my attention switched from the yellow light to the swiftness at which the door opened. I got hit by the sudden blast of cold air and saw a flurry of snow swirl into the mausoleum. It was then the strange haunting tune developed behind me for the first time. Maybe the tune was the call signal to the wolf. I heard the whistled notes calling the silver wolf, perhaps for some bestial ritual.

The silver wolf leapt into the open wooden hatch and came straight towards me. I saw its teeth, with the lips curled back and the flash of those yellow eyes looking like fires. Immediately my throat went dry and I clutched for the weapon I never possessed. My hands jerked towards my face in defence but something quite simple halted the savage wolf in its tracks. I, Mikhail, experienced the haunting tune once more. It was a continuation of that sound. I heard it, quite tinny and then the wolf shimmered. I gulped with surprise. The horror and expectation of the wolf attack melted away. I could only guess at what happened. I'd heard that which linked the shape-changing of the silver wolf into a domestic black dog. Because that was what I saw: a black dog...

My next shock came when I noticed Zacho the Russian Armenian dwarf standing there watching me. His once jovial face now could only be described as bestial; the eyes gave out that message. As I watched, the dwarf removed a silver whistle from his lips. Moments earlier when he'd blown it the sound had pierced the air, hurting my ears. That too was when I, Mikhail, first saw the silver wolf change with the whistle.

Zacho advanced towards me, his heavy looking arms reaching out for me already. I recognised him and saw the sharp long knife he held. He flicked his wrist: the knife rested at my throat. Another flick and the knife drew blood. The dwarf paused to smile. I jerked and bit my lip.

Carefully Zacho herded me back towards the deeper parts of the mausoleum. We went deeper and deeper still, until I advanced through a door, into a much bigger room in the recess of the mausoleum, maybe even under a building. Instinctively I knew what Zacho had done; he'd used his skills to dig out and furnish a place of his own. All the comforts existed for him; he was like a king enthroned. And the tale of the silver wolf would keep strangers away, except this time the story was true.

I feared the wolf but now it took the shape of a tame dog. It scampered around the dwarf and me. We kept going until we proceeded into a large room where the dog collapsed on a rug in front of the fire. Around the walls hung a series of thick candles. I was in a graveyard, so the candles didn't seem out of place but the light cast by them fuelled a haunting picture. The face of the dwarf made me shiver. Shiver. Then I thought of the dead man I'd uncovered earlier. Though I guessed at the worst, could I be right about Zacho? And what truth lay behind the tame dog? And the dead woman as well?

Zacho prodded me with his knife and kicked a chair toward me. I sat down. But the hospitality did not end there. Zacho pulled out a coil of rope and tied me to the wooden chair.

Once I offered no security threat, the dwarf hobbled around the room. He sharpened his knife once more and sliced up pieces of a human arm. I saw it, saw the rings on the fingers. I watched him toss food to the dog. I felt sorry for the dead victim, for the person I did not know.

Mindful of the position I was in, I also felt sorry for myself. I wondered about my Anna, about all her worry when I never returned last night. And then to my horror I noticed Anna's coat on the back of a chair. A bloodstained coat. I stared at it, as I feared the worst. So it really seemed as if the wolf killed Anna. I felt sick thinking of my wife. She should have done what I told her and stayed at home.

Somebody said all good things have an ending, so do bad things. Bearing such a thought in mind I knew sooner or later Zacho needed to eat me. His sharp knife always cut so well and I'd feel the pain. I guess I'd scream but nobody would hear me, not even the dwarf, as he was deaf as well as mute. I imagined him tossing my fingers to the dog/wolf and cutting steaks off me.

On the cooker lay several pots of steaming vegetables. I watched as the dwarf checked each pan. Eventually his inspection satisfied him. Presently he served a huge portion onto a plate and followed this by slices of meat drawn from his grisly supply. A graveyard always contained plenty of meat after all, and he exploited it to the full.

The black dog finished eating. It slouched away down the passage perhaps out into the snow-covered graveyard. Zacho didn't pay it too much attention but I watched that black dog. I couldn't help but wonder about it and my Anna when I should have tried to escape. Now I shared the place with only Zacho.

Zacho's face twisted into a smile as he poured out a glass of red wine. As he tried to feed it to me most of it spilt down my cheeks and ran down my neck. I gulped at the wine and used it to quench my thirst. Zacho too drank some. Soon he was red-faced and drunk. While he stayed in a stupefied state at least I remained alive.

Once he finished eating, Zacho cleared the table. He covered it with a large cloth. Now from within a leather case he drew out a short knife; this he proceeded to sharpen. I watched in fascination and yet still pondered my fate.

As I watched Zacho I kept an eye on the scruffy torn red coat he lifted from the back of a chair to wear. It was my Anna's coat, after all, and she was dead. I felt sick in my stomach. I wanted revenge and all I could do was watch him strut up and down wearing her coat.

Moments later I heard something coming closer and increasing in intensity. What I heard was related to our Ninth Kazanski Cossacks. The jangle of the harness didn't bother me anymore. I welcomed the sound of the Cossacks. Another relief came when I heard Boris shout my name.

Zacho took off the red coat and left it on the side to taunt me. He then started to sharpen his knives once more. I watched as he laughed to himself. I felt the chill as I realised Zacho was completely mad.

The speed at which the rescue took place astounded me. One minute I looked at Zacho and then he took two bullets in his chest as the Russian Cossacks burst down the door behind me. They swarmed into the room and kicked the dead Zacho. I cried out with relief and they released my bonds. I felt so stressed I didn't know whether to laugh or cry. I recognised Boris and shouted at him. He passed me a bottle of vodka and I drank half in one go. Then he took me back home. I, Mikhail Razumovsky, felt so cold without my Anna.

***

Two months later even though Anna was dead and buried I still thought of her. I took out her red coat, held it tenderly to my face as I thought of her. I ran my hand over the material and then put on the coat. Naturally it was too small but it was something I had to do. My hand slipped into a pocket and closed on a silver whistle. It was like the one Zacho used.

I took the coat off. I needed to examine the whistle for any marking but there was none. Even as I stood there, Boris came in, his face red with vodka. He brought some cold air into the house with him.

Boris greeted me in his usual way by breathing vodka fumes everywhere. Then he paused and lurched towards me.

"I'll take that," he said. "No good to you unless you can play." Then he pointed a finger at the far corner of the room. "Smart looking dog you have, Mikhail. When did you get it?"

I looked at where he indicated and gasped with disbelief. On the mat in the corner of the room lay the black dog. It had been there watching me and I hadn't noticed. Or did it come in with Boris? Before I could think properly or even answer, Boris took the silver whistle and placed it between his lips. He looked at my face and smiled. Then he must have seen my terror when I noticed the black dog up on its feet and growling.

I, Mikhail Razumovsky, watched as Boris, the drunk, blew the whistle...

Geordie Moore

"I tell you the witch doctor is back," Geordie Moore said. "I had those dreams again. Something is up. I'm scared. With red hair like mine and being unable to walk, I guess I'm crazy. Jinxed? Superstitious even. But I dreamt the guy killed people here. In this nursing home. I've never known it like this. So clear. In my head."

Geordie pulled at his hair with his fingers. His blue eyes lingered on Dr Stephen Lambert's face. He frowned at Jarge Benson who hoped to interview him outside in the fresh air. Geordie looked down at his 14 stone bulk and wondered when he'd walk again. He stared at his large belly, then at his large loose-fitting shoes. Being a film director hadn't stopped him getting fat or the ingrown toenails.

With his dream of walking fixed in his thoughts Geordie started when he heard the police sirens in the distance. An image leapt into his mind as the sirens got louder. He rubbed his lips with the back of his hands and paused for thought.

"The witch doctor; he's back in my dreams, Dr Lambert. And I'm in pain with these toenails of mine. I want out of this wheelchair; I want to walk. Maybe it's too soon after the operation. It's always bad luck with me, as if I've been cursed. The dreams are a backward step, aren't they?"

Dr Lambert smiled as he adjusted the red flower in the lapel of his suit. His youthful appearance, enthusiasm and style attracted many clients to his hypnotherapy practice.

"Geordie, half of what you say makes sense. Your fears make up the rest," Dr Lambert said. "I sorted your dreams out before using hypnosis. I can do that again. You do have bad luck, and I agree you should try walking. Be positive and you'll give Wendy a surprise. Please excuse me. I'll be back in a few minutes. I must find out what is happening with the police and all that."

Before he left a nurse entered the room. As she looked at

Geordie's file a black feather fluttered onto the floor. She sighed, picked up the feather and showed it to the doctor. His face went pale and he checked to see if Geordie had noticed it. Then the doctor and nurse left the room to the sound of approaching police sirens.

***

"Witch doctors and bad dreams," Geordie said. "It was why I saw Dr Lambert in the first place. After the dreams my local doctor thought I had MS, but the tests cleared me.

"Then I found it difficult to walk. Another check and the hospital discovered I had angina, asthma and ingrown toenails. That's my bad luck. The angina and asthma are sorted; the toenails have been removed and, though they hurt like hell, I'm planning on walking. You see I've a bride and wedding planned. Even though I'm no spring chicken at fifty-five. It's all because I met Wendy."

Sixty-year-old Jarge Benson listened, his black hair shot with grey. He was well known for his weather-beaten face and those twinkling eyes, so keen to focus on life's interesting details. A winning feature of Jarge was how well he related to people, and his bouncy nature.

"Congrats on the wedding. A curse? Go easy on that one. I know about curses," Jarge said. "Please believe me." His grim look stayed on his face when he said those words.

Even as Jarge asked questions for his interview, police activity increased in the grounds outside. Two uniformed officers entered Geordie's room and carried out a quick search.

"Stay calm. We are searching for an African dressed in a white robe," one policeman explained. "He's dangerous according to the Immigration Services. They arrested him for not having an ID card but he escaped into these grounds. Be on your guard if you see him."

As the police broadened their search they found more black feathers scattered across the site.

***

When Dr Lambert returned they talked about the police manhunt and its progress. As he spoke, the doctor took out photographs from his pocket. He spread the pictures onto the table quickly and arranged them in rows for easy viewing. Carefully the doctor pointed to each photo as he studied Geordie's face for reactions.

"See here. These are excellent shots. Well, they all are. Here is how you looked in my clinic the first time," Dr Lambert said. "Then with the false scare of MS. After that with angina, asthma and here after your toe operations. Forget the juju thing and curses. Think weddings. You'll soon be walking at Wendy's side."

Geordie went silent as he found breathing difficult. Quickly he used his aerosol for his asthma.

"Yep. Married bliss and me on my feet," Geordie said. "Bad luck? No way. Have walk. Will marry. My motto."

Dr Lambert smiled again. He glanced at their faces and then back again at the photos.

"Great stuff. I'm here to help. It's part of my job," Dr Lambert said. He got to his feet and left the room. As he walked across the lawn his eyes noted the extra security staff drafted in to help with the search. Something was serious. The doctor wondered about the ambulance surrounded by policemen. Then he thought about his own worry of the black feather.

***

Geordie amazed Jarge with a variety of tales during the interview. The details concerned the intrigue of a lifetime spent in the film industry and visiting locations around the world.

"When I found out the Marchinai tribe worshipped birds, I had to make a film of their life.

"Inside three months I returned to film in Gondas Menjarro, a mountainous region in Upper Volta. From there we made some documentaries.

"By chance I saw a cave painting. It was enough to set me off for a project. But when I returned from the UK things went wrong and kept going wrong.

"It was the bouts of depression I couldn't handle." Geordie paused in telling his tale. "I grabbed bottles of spirits and drove off into the bush for wild drinking sessions.

"The hours sped by. I might rest a little but I always kept drinking. At daybreak the next day I found myself heading towards our camp. I looked out for a campfire, a light, anything to guide me in. At that point I ran over something.

"I say something, because I couldn't be sure what it was, I was that drunk. It got squashed. I looked with a torch but there was nothing. All I found was a short strip of torn cloth.

"I put the cloth in my pocket and returned to the camp to sleep, I was that exhausted. I needed sleep.

"The next morning, there was a loud commotion in the camp. I awoke to find all the natives had deserted. I dressed quickly and darted into the camp where I bumped into a stranger. His evil looks scared our helpers away.

"The weird-looking man stood in front of the Land Rover, his black robes covered in all kinds of brown and black feathers. I noticed his hands, saw the rings and beads and watched how the gold jewellery contrasted with the colour of his skin.

"When he saw me he leapt high in the air doing long leaps. As he made these jumps he scattered red dust to make a dense fog.

"I stared into those fierce dark eyes and felt them bore into my soul. I shivered, in spite of the heat. Quickly his ritual ended and he pushed me towards the Land Rover. He chanted and pulled the strip of cloth from my pocket. I felt sick and turned away. When I looked back the juju man had gone.

"Twelve months later my bad dreams started. I saw Dr Lambert and he helped me through hypnosis. And then along came angina, asthma and ingrown toenails."

The interview ended. Jarge thanked the film director and left. Geordie got to his feet and rested his arms on the back of the wheelchair. His face changed. But not with the pain in his toes. He glanced down; saw the single black feather on the wheelchair cushion. The discovery made him sweat. He felt scared. He knew he couldn't run from the inexplicable so he spent quiet moments thinking about Wendy and his kismet. He became calm but positive as he stood there determined to walk that day.

Ten minutes later Dr Lambert walked into the room with Wendy Lisburne.

Outside the search continued, but louder than before. Men shouted as the security sweep went on throughout the nursing home. Two policemen entered Geordie's room to check again.

***

Wendy Lisburne possessed a special ability to dress simply and yet with a certain class. Her sleek black skirt showed off her figure, the Thai red blouse completed her sexy image. At thirty-five her looks, svelte figure and charm made her the ideal partner for film director Geordie Moore.

Her blonde hair, cut at shoulder length, always looked clean and fresh and moved easily when she turned her head. But besides her physical looks Wendy showed her compassion, love and sincerity in the charity work she did. It took a special sort of person to give up free time to work in a hospice for children. People discovered this when they found out more about her.

"Look at the photographs, Wendy," Dr Lambert encouraged. "See what you think. My next photo will show Geordie walking at your wedding. I know he can do it."

Wendy examined the pictures on the table.

"Oh, these are super. I know you are in pain, Geordie," Wendy said. "But it's our special day. Walk on the day and make me happy."

Geordie went quiet. Then he whispered to her and she smiled.

"Okay." Geordie said enthusiastically. "So as I'm up on my feet I'm going to walk outside. Now."

Minutes later, Geordie looked at Wendy and the look on her face as she encouraged him to take his first steps. He laughed and joked about getting discharged from the hospital.

"Go on across there," the policeman said. "Once we've cleared this side we've some dogs to do our searching for us." The police pointed to the spot where other staff and patients from the nursing home assembled.

Geordie kept an arm around Wendy as they walked slowly across the lawn towards the place indicated by the police. Dr Lambert followed a little behind them. Sometimes his eyes rested on the policemen. He listened to the throaty bark of a German Shepherd and then heard it answered by another.

Wendy went quiet. She stopped with a puzzled expression on her face. She clutched at Geordie's shirt and twisted it in her hands. Geordie looked at her; followed her gaze and wondered. Dr Lambert felt surprised too.

Everybody in the nursing home grounds looked up at the strange black dot in the sky. It became bigger as they watched. Every second provided them with more detail. Already they gauged its speed; saw it move closer overhead. Something about its simple blackness terrified them.

Geordie swallowed, then wanted to spit. An odd taste crept into his mouth. He couldn't place the feeling but guessed it was fear. He certainly felt sick but not with excitement. Maybe nausea. His hands went around Wendy for support as he waited.

More uniformed policemen ran onto the lawn. They looked up at the black cloud and were puzzled by the quantity of black feathers drifting down from it. Scarcely had the first feathers landed when the police dogs started barking. And kept barking.

***

Geordie saw how the black dot quickly developed into a tight formation of black vultures. To his surprise he heard the noise, the loud grunts, squawks, screeches and sensed the evil of the hideous birds. He tightened his grip on Wendy and tried to stop her from screaming.

Instinctively they and the doctor moved towards the nearest building for protection, away from the black shadow above. Wendy screamed as Geordie slipped and went down on one knee. He released her hand as he struggled to get to his feet.

In those few seconds something jerked movement into Geordie's body. Both Wendy and the doctor saw his body jump, then they saw him whisked up into the mass of the birds overhead. Wendy screamed. He disappeared from sight. At that point a cacophony of sound broke out as the birds flew off with Geordie. Wendy screamed again. Moments later the birds flew out of sight leaving a deep silence behind them.

Dr Lambert sweated. He was scared by what he'd just seen. It took him moments to think straight enough to get a nurse to look after Wendy. He'd seen something through the trees on the other side of the lawn. He ran.

"Over there, lads. Grab him. That's the man!"

Already the policemen shouted and the police dogs raced to attack the target in the trees. Dr Lambert followed behind them but nobody was quick enough.

The tall African man stood in white robes in the centre of the ring of trees. Dr Lambert guessed his identity from the descriptions he'd had from Geordie. The man held a head in his hand. It was easy to see it was Geordie's severed head from the colour of the hair. Seconds later the man shimmered and changed into a vulture. They saw it seize Geordie's head and take flight to join the other birds on the horizon. Then all the birds disappeared.

Nobody saw Geordie again, alive that is.

***

Hours later, the Metropolitan Police sent a car racing, sirens on, towards London Bridge. The police quickly encircled the set of iron railings when they saw the head impaled on the sharp spikes. The red hair and the ID card around the neck provided sufficient details for the initial identification.

The press exploited the chilling discovery. It wasn't only the severed head that attracted mass media attention; the findings of the post-mortem certainly did. Detective Inspector Keith Bradley, involved with the case, remained shocked when shown the inside of Geordie's skull.

"Look here. The brain has gone. All we have left is a pile of soft black feathers," the senior member of the autopsy team said to him. "I don't know what to make of it all."

***

Months later after Geordie's death, Wendy Lisburne gave birth to a baby boy. Wendy, thrilled with the birth of her son, only regretted that Geordie never saw him.

Dr Stephen Lambert visited Wendy, and with a smile he passed over flowers, grapes and cards. He too expressed his delight with the birth of the baby boy and mentioned Geordie by name.

Wendy was quiet as she wiped a tear from her eyes. She missed having Geordie by her side as a partner. Especially when everything about the baby boy was so perfect, even taking into account the ginger hair.

"Strange how things work out," the doctor said, "Geordie was so concerned with bad luck. His affliction. Now you have a splendid little baby with Geordie as the father. So, can we now forget about bad luck?"

Wendy nodded and watched as the doctor went to the window. She heard him gasp as he pulled back the curtains.

"My God. I don't believe it," Dr Lambert said loudly.

Wendy sat upright in the bed. She stared at where the doctor pointed.

Quickly she too sucked in her breath as she saw the dozens of black birds sitting on the fence outside. All were black, except for one with red feathers on one side of its body.

As the nurse entered the private room, the bird with red feathers flew straight at the window pane. It made a loud noise as it struck. Wendy screamed, remembering Geordie's 'bad luck.' Wendy screamed again.

When she stopped and looked the bird had gone...with the others, leaving behind a single red feather on the window ledge.

The Indian Rope Trick

"Get Ali Baba up there; make him let us in," Egidio insisted. "Any mistake and I shoot."

Mafia boss Egidio Bellucci pulled out his gun. He waved it skyward at the open second-floor window. "Five million pounds in bonds waiting for us and you messed up the ladder. Better pray we get in, otherwise I get nasty." Egidio tapped his wristwatch with his gun.

Stefano gulped and took over. So the ladder broke when he put his weight on it, but pasta was his God, as his waistline testified. In sheer desperation to find a way to access the small window, Stefano dived into his magazine of ideas. He worked hard. He thought finding the Jerry Cottrell Circus performer Gopal Sangur Singh waiting at a bus stop was a lucky break for him. It took only a moment to kidnap the friendly yet naïve Indian. Now all that was needed was entry to the office block through the open window. Soon he and his boss Egidio would be in the money.

Fat Stefano watched Gopal, noting the *dhoti* and the sleeveless cotton jacket the Indian wore. No sandals covered his feet, yet around his head he sported a bright blue turban. Gopal carried a flute in his right hand and a wicker basket under his other arm.

Stefano raised a foot and kicked the basket. As the basket fell, the lid came off and spewed out a length of heavy rope. Gopal looked down at it.

"Come on! Pick it up!" Stefano shouted. "I need you to do your stunt and get your rope up to that window. When you get there I want you to slip in and let us into the room. A friend has left a key on the desk so there should be no problem. You understand?"

"Yes, Sahib. I speak damn bloody good English, sir."

Soon they would be in the offices of Wardle, McCarthy & Company and so rich. Egidio had bribed an office worker to leave a window open and to provide a handy key to the security door.

The Indian picked up the sprawling rope and wound it into a neat looking coil before placing it back inside the wicker basket. He wet his lips and fingered the holes on the slim flute. Stepping back a little, he dropped to the ground and folded his brown legs into the familiar yoga pose. Tight-lipped, Stefano listened as Gopal started to play.

Gopal played some weird cranky tune for half a minute, but nothing happened. Stefano, however, saw a slight movement within the basket. He heard a peculiar friction sound as the coil of rope moved around and next spiralled upwards. Gopal played on, driving the rope upwards towards the heavens in tune with the music. Stefano glanced up, grunting with delight as the rope snaked past the open window.

"Stop!" Stefano shouted and pointed. "Now climb the rope and do what I said. Get that key off the desk and let us in. Go now. Hurry. Hurry."

Gopal Sangur Singh did nothing for a long moment. Finally he arose and his hands reached up for the rope. His brown legs entwined around the length of it as he began his smooth and steady climb. Stefano watched in amazement as the man climbed up until he was level with the open window on the second floor.

***

'Boy' Fletcher wasn't drunk at the time, but he felt as if he was. The ex-alcoholic saw, from an adjacent office, Gopal climb up level with his window. Immediately 'Boy's chest started heaving, sweat glistened on his forehead as he dropped to the floor, his back against a wall for reassurance. As he fiddled with his mobile phone, he became worried as to what to say and who would believe his story.

He was a man of forty-two but somehow looked many years younger. It was for that reason he got his nickname of 'Boy'. He'd tried in the past to stop being called 'Boy' but somehow the tag stayed with him. Now as he opened a can of beer and took a drink he felt slightly better. Seeing Gopal had been a shock but the beer helped. He rang a number on the mobile phone again and when he spoke of what he saw his speech sounded slurred.

***

Carefully, Gopal reached inside the small open window. He turned the latch to the side window, the larger one big enough to give him access. As it opened, Gopal stepped across the threshold and went into the room. He disappeared from sight.

Egidio joined Stefano and the two men watched in half amazement at the rope still hanging above them. It didn't occur to them that what they saw was no trick. Greed was enough to dull their sense of wonder.

Presently the door to the building opened and Gopal stood there.

As the two men rushed inside, Gopal picked up his basket and fed the rope back inside it. He had finished coiling the rope and replaced the lid on the basket when Stefano returned.

"Come on. The boss wants you upstairs," Stefano said. Gopal picked up his basket and followed Stefano.

In that short space of time Egidio and Stefano located the bonds they needed. Now they had Gopal, they made use of him to fill black bags with the bonds they took from various drawers. The insider information was excellent; it enabled them to find the bonds very quickly as they emptied several large security containers.

***

Less than fifteen minutes later Egidio was closer to his dream of getting rich than he'd ever imagined possible. The bags containing the bonds were loaded up in the back of their Range Rover.

Egidio stood in the yard outside smoking a cigarette. Stefano joined him minutes later. Both men looked at their watches.

"Time to go, boss. But what about Ali Baba upstairs? What are we going to do with him? Heck, I could do with a drink."

Egidio hunched his shoulders. With millions hanging in the balance he didn't want any mistakes.

"Best shoot him. One bullet in the head should do it."

Stefano nodded and checked his gun. He climbed up the stairs to carry out his orders.

As he entered the room, a glance showed him Gopal sitting cross-legged on the floor. Stefano guessed he was meditating as the man kept both eyes shut. This part was going to be easy.

Stefano pressed the trigger and Gopal slumped to the floor, a trickle of blood showing the place where the bullet entered his head. A second later the mobster holstered his gun and went down the stairs.

***

'Boy' Fletcher heard the shot. He peeped out of the window. Everything was quiet but the sound of the shot worried him. What had happened to the Indian man up there in the air? 'Boy' returned to his mobile phone and tried again.

***

Stefano left the room with Gopal motionless on the floor. But the Indian was not dead. Tiny parts of his lungs were still working, keeping him alive. Something inside his brain stopped him from dying. Eventually, an aura hovered over the body of the Indian. A mystical entity withdrew from it. Only those adepts gifted in the art would have seen the wondrous thing move from Gopal's body and into the wicker basket.

As the two men were leaving the office building, they heard a noise coming from the room where Gopal lay dead. The strange sound made them freeze in their tracks, only their eyes lifted towards the upstairs office.

"I said to kill him," Egidio said.

Stefano shuffled his feet.

"I did."

"So what was that sound? He's walking about. Get up there quick and check it out. We need to get out of here pretty soon. When you are up there grab that last pile of bonds I left on the main desk by mistake. I thought they were worthless but apparently that isn't so. Now jump to it. Okay?"

Stefano nodded. He took out his gun and climbed the stairs. As he entered the room, he found Gopal hadn't moved a fraction from where he'd been shot. Stefano kicked him and felt for a pulse. He found none.

Stefano remembered what Egidio said about the bonds. He picked up the wicker basket, emptied the rope onto the floor and rested the basket on the desktop. Immediately Stefano grabbed at the bonds and threw them into the wicker basket. When he finished he moved towards the door.

As he held the wicker basket in front of him, ready to make the descent down the stairs, something slid across the floor. Once it focused on him it struck at high speed like an Exocet missile.

Stefano felt the first fierce tug as it wrapped around his legs, pulling until it threw him off balance. He screamed once as he hopped right at the top of the staircase. He struggled, he trembled and lost the battle as the rope raced around his ankles to pitch him forward with only a wall to cushion his blow. The basket dropped from his lifeless hand.

***

Egidio paused. He heard the slight commotion. “Stefano. Don’t mess about. Come on let’s get out of here.” There was no answer to his shout.

In one smooth move, Egidio took his gun out and climbed the stairs, pausing at each third step to listen. Before he got to the top he saw Stefano’s twisted body. Egidio’s eyes moved from the head wound to the wicker basket and the bonds scattered on the stairs.

The gang boss shrugged his shoulders and picked up the basket. As he climbed the stairs Egidio kept collecting the bonds. He took the basket into the office and placed it on the desk.

Within seconds of entering the office, Egidio saw the dead Indian. The shock of also seeing Stefano, dead on the stairs, blood pouring from a head wound spooked Egidio. He shuddered but pressed on. He went back to Stefano’s body. As he searched through the dead man’s pockets, Egidio came across more money. Back in the office Egidio added the money to the wicker basket. He pulled on the lid and tried to lift the basket off the desk.

Egidio’s instincts cried out a warning inside his head. The basket was too heavy. It was too strange. With his gun he levered off the lid. As the lid jerked and fell to the floor, sweat broke out on his face and hands. He sprang back, his gun ready, his eyes riveted on the inside of the basket.

Egidio made the mistake of seeing the snake with haunting yellow eyes rear up in front of him. It was too late for him to fire. He knew that, when the venom hit him in the eyes, making him drop his gun. Even as he clutched his face, the cobra struck again. Within seconds, Egidio felt himself reacting, his body going into convulsions, until he soon dropped to the floor.

The snake ignored Egidio’s body; instead it went and found the dead Gopal. Picking a spot alongside the dead man the snake wound itself into a tight coil. It held the position for several minutes. Soon an aura developed around the snake. As the intensity of the shimmering aura increased a spirit moved from the snake to Gopal.

Almost at once Gopal started to breathe again. His chest started to rise and fall. Though his breathing was slow and laborious, he was alive.

***

When the paramedics found Gopal, they discovered by his side a neat coil of thick rope. They discovered more money inside the wicker basket but found no sign of any snake. But some evidence indicated that Egidio died from a snakebite.

***

'Boy' Fletcher, the ex-drunk, happened to be still stuck in a position overlooking the yard. Naturally he phoned the Thames Valley Police after he'd drunk a few cans of beer to steady his nerves. Anybody would have done the same.

Especially if they'd seen an Indian climbing up a huge thirty-foot long cobra with large yellow eyes...

Goo

Good old St. George, he had slain the Dragon...but did he ever dream of what he had unleashed as dragon blood stained the battlefield?

England needs more than a banner to rally around in this hour of need...Listen. Listen. I beg you.

Certain events have gone terribly sour on me and I believe I must write down everything now in the hope that anyone who listens to me will understand, and take action. My name is Jeff Slater, though if this scourge isn't stopped soon, names will be meaningless. Ours is a dying planet...

It all began when I left Rhone-Poulenc to work for G. S. Carlton of Faringdon, who needed a graduate biochemist able to analyse some green stuff seeping out of the ground at a place called Dragon Hill at Uffington.

The work was routine but full of interest. I discovered that British SESCOL had drilled for oil at roughly the same location two years ago, making me suspect they had unknowingly upset some delicate balance of nature.

From my lessons on history and mythology at school, I also know Dragon Hill was where St. George fought and killed the dragon. It was on the famous hill at Uffington in Oxfordshire a lot of dragon blood was spilt...

For many months I worked on the problem, but all I know is that the seepage is super organic matter with strange three-pronged units that operate in complex manoeuvres. It's not blood; that would be too easy but I know they tend to link up like a child's toy pack of building bricks.

Experiments I did revealed the goo was a powerful fertiliser capable of accelerating the growth of crops. Its origin always remained a mystery to me.

I completed a report with full recommendations. It was accepted since it offered a product with huge potential. The directors of G. S. Carlton made millions, and I got pretty rich as well. But I was uneasy – a natural reaction, I believe, when something seems too easy – and although I couldn't characterise it, I felt something was not so much wrong as not quite right. My new wealth freed me from the necessity of daily toil, so I decided to continue with private research on the goo.

For a long time all was quiescent. Then I developed an excruciating pain in my navel and the surrounding skin began swelling. Naturally, on noticing it in the shower I prodded the aggravated area with my fingertips; disconcertingly, as a result the skin split, and out shot a small grotesque green foot! It kicked, as if controlled by a mind of its own.

My nerve snapped when I saw the hideous member as I could not catalogue it as belonging to any animal I knew. Even in this relatively enlightened age, I wanted to hide my sudden affliction from others. But the scientist in me was curious, so I determined to analyse the foot.

I cut a sliver of skin from it for a slide. I was emboldened when I realised I felt no pain. Under the 'scope, I detected the familiar three-pronged unit I'd come across in researching the goo. This wasn't blood but complex DNA structure of a type I'd never seen before. It was enough to make me shudder.

At about the same moment my girlfriend, Susan Laker, called. To make an understatement, I was at a low ebb and confided in her regarding my predicament. She thought I was joking until I revealed the monstrous thing. She advised me to get medical help at once. After a while, I managed to convince her we might be on the verge of something 'big' concerning the goo, as I termed it. A foot on its own is no good according to the old fashioned way I thought, so can it be more sophisticated DNA and RNA cells than we can imagine? This was the first alien thing I'd encountered and it puzzled me. Is the foot a kind of genetic pack to be assembled at the right time? Was an activator or catalyst needed? (See the Appendix to this report on reactions). But what was driving me crazy was trying to work out the nature of the beast.

Then I had a pain in my chest followed by the eruption of a small green claw! There were no fingernails, all the digits were the same in size and it had no thumb. We both watched in horror as it pulled at my body, as if trying to release itself.

I've talked it over with Susan, and I've agreed to make this taped report for you, our MP. Why you? Well, this strange effect must be connected with the goo. I've eaten food grown on the stuff like countless thousands, if not millions. A local GP wouldn't be able to cope, I'm sure this is too big; it needs the government to act, and now. I guess it's true; you are what you eat...

***

The report continued, giving details of experiments. But Detective Inspector Duncan Evans of Faringdon had heard enough. He turned over the tape to his uncle, Chief Constable Alistair Quigley.

Duncan was an athletic-looking man of twenty-nine, fair-haired with a fresh complexion, and until hearing Slater's report, he'd always been smiling. No longer did his blue eyes smile however, the light had gone from his face; clearly, his concern showed.

"Duncan, there've been a lot of reports of this strange manifestation – the minister's wife, and Mary's got it now." Alistair blew his nose into a paper handkerchief. "The doctors want to amputate and she's scared."

"Good God, Alistair, I'm - sorry to hear…"

"Obviously the boffins are looking at the situation, closely monitoring, testing - but we need to talk to this Slater, he may know more than we've been able to glean from the report you've listened to..."

"Why send me, though? Surely the local bobby could go around to Slater's?"

"True. But, even with the outbreak spreading, we're trying to keep a lid on it. Of course, it's only a matter of time before it leaks and there's wholesale panic. Bring Slater in, Duncan."

Susan Laker was blonde, about twenty-five, he guessed as she answered the door.

"So they've finally decided to send someone round!" she said in exasperation. Ushering him in, she added: "Though it's probably too late by now..." She was pale, with dark rings under her blue eyes.

"Where is he?"

"He said something about visiting the Folly to think."

"There's certainly plenty to think about!"

"Don't blame him, Inspector. I made such a mistake, it's why we had a blazing row, and it's why he's gone to the Folly."

In the background the Carlton factory's muffled grumble was suddenly silenced. At last, instructions from on high had stopped the production of more goo.

Duncan left his car at the car park by the Folly Tower and started walking to the entrance; but before he could reach it a woman nearby screamed. He looked up in time to see a man's body plummet from the top of the 140-ft tower.

Immediately Duncan verified the dead man was Slater by checking through his pockets for credentials. Apart from the ID, Duncan noticed a tiny green appendage still moving under the clothing which confirmed his own thoughts on Slater's identity.

Duncan quickly covered the body with an old rug from his car, then called for backup. When the uniformed police arrived he showed his credentials and, accompanied by a constable, he climbed to the top of the tower. No foul play was suspected, but he'd better check.

Almost as soon as they stepped out onto the stone terrace at the top, they saw the bloody stump of a small green claw; its fingers still twitching as it gripped the balcony's iron rail.

"Hell," the young constable exclaimed. "It beats ET." His attempt at jocularity failed and he turned away to be sick.

Tentatively, Duncan wrapped the claw in a handkerchief.

He left instructions for the pathology people, emphasising the need for a speedy post-mortem. He tried contacting the Chief Constable but he was unavailable, so he decided to go home.

Duncan's wife Fiona and his son, Mark, were still on holiday in Dorset, so the house was austere, cold and unwelcoming, even though the sun shone outside.

As he heated some beans, he opened a window for fresh air, not wishing to smell the house out with burnt toast. While he ate beans on toast, topped with a fried egg against his better judgement, he watched golf on the small portable TV in the kitchen.

Annoyingly, the picture went fuzzy. He was unable to correct the fault. He switched off and in the sudden silence he noticed the Carlton plant had started up again, though louder.

Turning on the radio in an attempt to catch more of the golf, he found instead his favourite music, Tchaikovsky's *Pathetique*. He closed the window to blot out the intruding Carlton racket, but the noise seemed to get louder still.

Outside, some children played on the grass, others rode bicycles on the pavements and keen gardeners, glad of the sunshine, were busy tidying their flowerbeds. A few cars passed through the estate.

Nothing seemed out of place.

Then came a deep-throated *whoomph*!

A dense black smoke-cloud rose into the air from the direction of the Carlton factory. Something had triggered an explosion but whatever caused it became a secondary worry as people fought for their lives. Nobody had noticed the factory operating again until it was too late.

The radio buzzed with static, but was still audible; a news-flash on the local radio announced an airliner crash in Regent Street, London; there were multiple pile-ups; people losing control, killing others...death…blood…chaos...reports flooded in from around the world.

Movement outside distracted him. Men, women and children were rolling in agony on the ground. Their screams grew louder as they clutched their bodies. On the road, a passing car crashed and trapped the occupants.

Abruptly, the radio went dead, but he hardly noticed. Above the noise of chaos came a high-pitched whistle; it went on and on. Duncan started to walk and every step he took gave him pain. He rubbed his stomach but this wasn't nausea...

Panic made Duncan break into a sweat.

Before he could reach the bathroom an eruption came from his navel and sharp pains in his chest; instinctively he touched the green things growing from his body, felt blood, hot and sticky, his own blood. He retched, supporting himself against the doorjamb.

Even as he struggled with the handle and opened the door, something hot – very hot – exploded on the back of his neck with a peculiar sucking sound.

In that split second he saw reflected in the bathroom mirror his own horrified face as a hideous green probe reared upon his neck. Its tip ended in a bulbous head with tiny red eyes and large pointed ears. He was frozen in shock as a set of savage jaws curled around to greet his throat. They grew bigger and bigger!

Everything was still, deathly still. Then there was the sound of bones breaking. And flaming, dragon things, alien and wet, wriggled out to clamber over his motionless body to click into position.

They slithered from the room leaving behind trails in blood…and goo.

Dragon's Needles

England's 'Old Peculier' made the *Red Dragon* pub famous but Dudley and Verona found the atmosphere far more exciting than the strong beer. As new owners of the large manor house on Coxwell Road, they were proud of its tall chimneys and Victorian-style garden. Some two months later, after settling in, they checked out the town to see what it offered. The local pub seemed a good place to visit first.

While in the friendly pub, Dudley and Verona discussed their future plans. After the hectic pace of the previous months, they could take it easy knowing their new house was decorated exactly as they wanted it. Dudley also called in experts to sort out minor building problems, especially those associated with some of the arched windows. Now it was time for them to relax.

"Nice to see you unwind a little after all that hard work on the house. I mean the last year hasn't been too good for both of us. My health problems, and you with that woman Judith Vinney. Is she still causing trouble?"

"No, but she did try very hard. In the end, Phillip Chambers, our Company Chairman made her leave ETRES. That pleased us all. I thought I was the only guy she wanted to seduce, but I was wrong. Last time I saw her was maybe more than a year ago. Look, let's forget the old crow. She doesn't mean a thing to me. Come on, give the cider a go. Let's celebrate our house purchase and kids in the future. Now what colour scheme do we go for in the nursery, Verona?"

As they sat in the pub they enjoyed the cheerful fire, the drink and talking to the regulars. It was the combination of all those factors they felt would draw them back to the *Red Dragon.* They both agreed on that point. Especially after tasting 'Old Peculier'.

Dudley got to his feet and went to the bar to order more drinks. He pushed back his lank dark hair and then with a smile hooked a thumb inside his leather belt. He smiled knowing his extra weight was due to Verona's good cooking but his broad shoulders and trim stomach reflected his love of sport especially football and swimming.

Verona, too, liked to keep fit. Somewhere in the house the many lycra suits and tights told a story of aerobic classes, as did the exercise bike in front of the television. When she wore her favourite pink shell suit it contrasted with her long brown hair, often tied in a ponytail. Her green eyes and long eyelashes always drew attention as did the way she walked. At thirty-five she was two years younger than Dudley but because they kept fit they both appeared younger than their true age. A recent holiday in Malta had given them both a superb suntan.

The stone Cotswold fireplace dominated the room where the regulars gathered for their pints of beer. Across the chimney surround hung a polished teak board with a collection of eleven corn dollies suspended from individual hooks. There should have been thirteen, if the two empty hooks were anything to go by…

It was seeing the corn dollies for the first time prompted Dudley to question the old man gazing at the fire, but he appeared to be deaf. Then after a very long pause the old man approached them as if he'd remembered the question.

"You must be living in the 'Needles'," the old timer whispered in a gruff voice. " 'Dragon's Needles'."

Dudley and Verona were surprised by the way he emphasised the weird phrase 'Dragon's Needles'. His reply puzzled them. Perhaps he meant the house they'd purchased, since its tall chimneys gave a threatening impression when seen against a night sky. They looked almost like clawing fingers reaching for the ghostly moon. But 'Dragon's Needles?' What an odd name for a house. Then Dudley looked at the corn dollies again and wondered...about them.

A little research showed the old house had indeed been called 'Dragon's Needles', but to make an easier sale the strange name got dropped many years ago. The old man in the pub knew the house, and he certainly was familiar with the number thirteen carved on a beam in an upstairs room. Whenever Dudley and Verona visited the pub the old man always unfolded a little more information. It was enough to whet their appetite.

They learnt from the old man how historic Faringdon, situated between Oxford and Swindon, revealed its link with dragons when Roman engineers constructed the wooden fort on Folly Hill. Historians recorded an incident in which a ferocious dragon attacked and killed thirteen elite Roman soldiers. The soldiers of the Phalebus Corps became famous when a local stone mason carved pictograms on a slab depicting matchstick men pursued by a dragon.

***

A few months later, Dudley and Verona returned home at night, after a theatre visit, to see a light in an upstairs window. They knew the house was empty. Could it be thieves? Immediately Dudley stopped the car before the sound could alert anybody within the house.

The shape and position of the window puzzled him a great deal, especially when the builders had bricked up the original opening at the time they bought the house. They had done so at his request. But it was also arched unlike any other windows in the house. It reminded him of the stained-glass windows he'd seen in churches, the ones that showed St. George with his raised sword killing the legendary dragon.

From the window drifted an occasional puff of coloured smoke. Sometimes the smoke was red, sometimes yellow. It was the smoke that made him think of fire and many associated dangers.

"I'm going to find out what's happening," Dudley whispered. "Quick as you can, call the police on your mobile. Tell them about the intruders and the fire. Do it now!"

Dudley entered the house leaving Verona on her own. She called the police and prayed they'd come quickly. Her eyes remained fixed on the window as she listened to the wind, sounding like a demented daemon, blast through the trees. The garden, clad in darkness, made her tense, providing her with bizarre images. And then there was the fascination of the window.

Bright lights. A car stopped behind her and a leggy blonde jumped out. Verona wound down the car window as the woman ran to her.

"Where the hell is Dudley?" came the screech. Verona recognised Judith Vinney. "I've got to see him now," Judith demanded. She breathed hard, her face flushed with anger.

"But why? What's the game? Dudley's got nothing to do with you. So why chase him?" Verona sat upright; alert. She felt angry. Judith's appearance meant trouble; Verona wondered at what the truth might be.

"He's gone and made me pregnant, see! The bastard."

"What? What do you mean! You slut! You Jezebel! Don't walk

away from me. Let's settle this now!" Verona shouted and started to get out of the car but already Judith was on her way towards the house.

"Don't worry, I'll find him," Judith retorted over her shoulder.

Verona, alone again, heard the door to the house slam. She glanced up at the window and saw a shadow flicker across the curtains followed by another shadow. Had Judith found Dudley? It was too much for her to sit there and endure. Immediately she leapt out of the car and ran towards the house, close behind Judith. Verona felt so incensed she hadn't worked out what she'd do if she caught up with the woman. But she knew it was the passion she felt that drove her on. And if Dudley was delayed, she wanted to know what was behind it....

The door creaked as she entered the hall, though she tried to be quiet. The lights didn't work when she tried the switch. The whole house was in complete darkness and as she stumbled around she brushed up against furniture and objects. She smelt a candle and guessed it must have been extinguished by the sudden draught from the door opening. It was too hazardous to continue and it puzzled her when she'd been so close behind Judith. Verona stopped and retraced her steps back to the car. A quick search and she found a small torch. She returned and went into the house again.

As Verona shone the torchlight, it revealed old carpets and furniture; she could also tell by the musty smell, by her touch. The surreal experience gripped her, making her tremble as she leant against the door opening; she needed to rest to regain her energy. She felt she'd wandered onto a film set, not a part of her new house. She gulped when she saw the lilies in the vase; they were not her favourite flowers. Neither was the scent, it reminded her of graveyards. In fact the scent made her sick. Again her inner voice warned her of danger but she had to find Dudley. Then her eyes caught the crack of light from the room with the beam marked with the number thirteen.

Moments later, she turned the handle of the door and went in cautiously, seeing rows of chairs and a table covered with a rich purple cloth. The cloth bore a large drawing of a pentagram; on it lay a shiny-handled knife. She noticed strange symbols of an old or foreign origin on the handle.

At each end of the table stood a large lighted candle, like some sentinel of evil. The candles were set in holders made up of a cluster of thirteen serpent heads. By each candle stood a white saucer. Verona noticed one of the saucers was filled with a red liquid. What had she stumbled upon?

She coughed as the incense drifted towards her and felt the pressure of strong hands wrap around her body. She screamed when, in turning her head, she saw the robed women who held her and screamed louder still as they closed in on her, forcing her to one end of the table. In minutes the strange initiation 'rituals' were completed; a second white saucer was filled with red liquid and an ancient Roman symbol drawn on her forehead. The evil power symbol created Verona, the vixen with blazing green eyes. Now she craved revenge as a wronged woman...

But the 'Dragon's Needles' paid the price for being empty for so long; a rampant thirst for fulfilment arose in Judith and Verona. They both needed Dudley to become their spawn. And for the thirteen women in the now full coven, atonement was close at hand...

***

Dudley dashed into the house with a heavy spanner in his hand. He hesitated with surprise to see the inside of the house was almost unrecognisable. But he daren't stop. He couldn't find the stairs. The lights wouldn't work, and as he blundered about he suddenly found himself outside in the garden. The back door slammed shut. He cursed aloud. His bad luck trying to find his way in the dark had forced him into the orchard at the back of the house. There he found an old wooden ladder to escape from the Victorian garden by climbing over the surrounding brick wall.

He was puzzled by the time he reached the front of the house and very surprised to see the two cars. One car was his, of course, and the other he recognised as Judith's Honda. It prompted the question of what did her visit mean?

And where was Verona? And indeed what about the police? They should have arrived by now after Verona's call. He bit his lip as he wondered if he faced a night of confrontation? He didn't know.

"Oh God! Help me. Dudley! Dudley! Dudley!"

He heard Verona scream, so he raced back to the house. The light from the room upstairs now showed him the way. He ran up the steps and straight into the room. He gasped with the effort. As he paused, the thirteen women pounced and held him tight. He felt their long fingernails digging into his flesh. His struggle to escape seemed futile.

He screamed in horror as the knife-edge moved in towards his body. His eyes fixed on the keen edge of the blade. He pleaded for mercy but Verona and Judith looked at him with the same feverish delight as the other women. Steadily they moved him along the table. Behind him the door slammed. Soon he heard the heavy bolts rattle, and the click as a key turned in the lock. Quickly the women ripped his clothes off, to hold him in a cloud of incense. As they did so he heard a murmur, a mumbling, and an ancient incantation, all suggesting a frenzied request by the women. When their prayers ended Dudley became their prize.

***

A day later, some of the many American visitors who came to Faringdon each year called in at the *Red Dragon* pub. One such visitor remarked on the thirteen corn dollies hanging on their individual hooks over the Cotswold stone fireplace. Nobody knew where the two extra ones came from, or how they came to be stained. If they knew at all, they were certainly not saying. All the Americans showed a real interest in old English pub traditions and happily studied the old stone fireplace.

The scene was set with a log fire burning briskly in the hearth. Right in front of the fire sat an old man drinking his pint of 'Old Peculier.' The Americans who visited the *Red Dragon* with their Faringdon relatives also enjoyed their drinks and the splendid atmosphere. As they did so they couldn't help but notice how the old man stared into the fire, seeing images that could tell their own story. It was clear his mind was miles away, perhaps in those halcyon days of old when witches roamed the land.

"Say what do you call thirteen dolls, old buddy?" a tall American drawled. "Must be a name for them!" Michael J. Lee was curious about the corn dollies as he came from Window Rock where the Navajos made straw figures to sell. He watched in fascination as a small brown-eyed woman stepped forward and aimed her digital camera at the display.

"I came all the way from Cornwall," the woman said, "to get a photo for my article. I edit a newsletter for the Guild of Straw Craftsmen. If you're interested in folklore, check out a local ritual called 'Crying the Neck.' " She smiled and handed him a business card.

The old man looked at them all in a slightly puzzled way and adjusted his hearing aid. Maybe he wasn't hearing them right? Maybe what they asked didn't matter? But he kept looking at the thirteen corn dollies for a very long time. Eventually he spoke in a sad voice.

" 'Dragon's Needles'," he croaked. And then as if they hadn't heard him the first time he spoke more loudly. " 'Dragon's Needles'." He spoke again in his rich country accent and the Americans understood the few words he spoke. But what struck them as odd was why he rolled his eyes as he said those words.

And why the blood on two of the corn dollies looked so red and still wet...to the touch.

Yellow Moonstone

Moonlight flooded the pathway to the temple of the Shan Dragon in old Burma.

As Yente Sheng, the thief, sped along he could only think about the fabulous Yellow Moonstone he planned to steal, and the woman Jayna Kan who seduced him into making the attempt. Her sensuous body and soft red lips made him yield to her advances. Now Yente kept his thoughts on his reward and carried on running.

The animal sounds of the night filled Yente's ears. A strange roar drowned out the extravaganza of noises in the dense jungle. He knew it was no tiger but could it be the Shan Dragon? It was unlike any animal sound he had heard before.

He paused for a few moments outside the pagoda temple and looked up at the dark roof. He watched a few leaves drift down as he continued thinking about his mission. He shivered and yet the air was not cold.

The entrance was easy to find from the words Jayna used to describe the doorway to the temple.

"Imagine two stone elephants facing each other and standing up on their back legs," Jayna Kan had told him. "On top of the elephants are two tigers and on top of them a single goat. The door is situated between the front legs of the elephants."

Yente smiled to himself as he prepared to enter the Shan Temple.

***

The estate where the Dutchman Jacob Jan Luyken lived earned a reputation for producing more rubber per acre than any other. It was the success of the owner that drew Yente to meet Luyken and to find out how to finish off his thesis.

From the start Yente enjoyed the hospitality offered to him. He went to many social gatherings and got invited to many more. He enjoyed the music recitals and loved meeting interesting people. Best of all he liked to listen to stirring tales of the British Empire and how problems got solved in the past. The food and the ample supply of brandy at the evening gathering made life for the commerce student most enjoyable.

A memorable day came when Yente met the svelte Jayna Kan. Almost instantly he felt captivated by her butter brown skin and almond eyes, not forgetting the seductive effect of her cupid bow outlined in red. He related well with the Burmese woman who worked in an office on the estate. She too seemed drawn by his good looks. A few dates and he became bewitched by her charm and more open to the suggestions she made. It was not long before he slept with her but it was Jayna who dominated. When he needed her most she asked a favour and promised him much more than herself.

"I want you to do something for me," Jayna said. Her shapely hands, with their long red fingernails found and rested on her hips. She played with the fastening to her skirt and fluttered her heavy-lidded eyes as she awaited his reply. He loved the glistening colours of her eyeliners when she blinked.

"Anything," Yente replied. And from that moment he knew he was hooked. He wanted her body.

"There is a jewel," she said softly. "You must get it for me. It's in an unguarded temple. Do that and I'm yours."

That conversation occurred a week ago. Jayna had planned everything and now he stood deep in the jungle outside the Shan Temple.

***

When Yente entered the temple, he noticed the contrast; outside the bright moonlight, now he faced a dark, sinister and foreboding interior. The scavenging beetles didn't help his nerves. Neither did the scuttling rats. So what was really happening? His feet loudly trod through bone-dry paper and rubbish.

The floor ahead of Yente seemed black and shiny. His torch showed thousands of cockroaches covering it in a dense carpet. He tried but it was impossible to avoid them or not hear the crunching sound at every step he took.

Now his torchlight found the awesome statue of the Shan

Dragon. It towered over him, and quickly he mounted the rich teak pedestal and used his penknife to prize out the jewel from the gold band around the neck of the dragon. He dropped the jewel into his shirt pocket and jumped down from the pedestal; he was off.

As he steered his way towards the exit and across the mass of cockroaches, fear lent wings to his feet as he felt a sudden nervous reaction down his spine. He broke into a sweat as he paused for breath. The pause made him remember the curse. Ancient Burmese folklore told of the Shan Dragon that has many friends. It was a warning he should have heeded. Images as deep as the Burmese jungle emerged from his subconscious to frighten him. He was so scared. What had he started? His imagination ran riot: it fuelled his inner fears as he puzzled over the unguarded sacred dragon temple and the ease with which he had stolen the Yellow Moonstone.

Before he emerged from the temple, he heard large bodies falling outside. He listened and heard the trumpeting of elephants. Moments later the roar of tigers startled him, as they sounded so close. He hid behind the door and peeped out.

To Yente's surprise he found the two stone elephants had gone. The tigers on their shoulders had also vanished. From the depths of the jungle he heard the chatter of monkeys and half imagined something black moved in the branches above his head. Perhaps a panther, but he couldn't be sure. Once again his imagination ran wild, driven on by the suggestive strange curse.

He shivered. Minutes later as he progressed along the path he tapped his shirt pocket. As he did so he discovered it empty. No. He must go back. Now. He could only have dropped the jewel in his flight from the temple. It must be somewhere along the moonlit footpath.

Yente started back, aware of his pounding heart and the now louder sounds of the night. What was the haunting echo? He guessed at the Shan Dragon but surely it didn't exist. He looked up. Just above the line of trees something moved with beating wings. Perhaps...

It was enough to play on his nerves and he couldn't even put a name to it. Ahead, a tiger stopped to look at him before it crossed the path and disappeared into the gloomy jungle. An enraged elephant sounded a trumpet call, followed in seconds by the dense black cloud of bats that clicked and squealed at him.

Unexpectedly a goat appeared from nowhere, it brushed him aside as it galloped past. He got to his feet in time to see the goat as it vanished through the trees into the Burmese jungle, like the tiger. The goat missed him by inches but it had been close. Yente, the thief, breathed hard and continued, with the words of the curse ringing in his ears.

Next came an assault of mosquitoes as they buzzed around him. He felt the pinpricks they made and the irritation. He beat the insects off with his hands as he wondered what was happening. Then as quickly as they appeared the mosquitoes vanished. He looked around. Immediately he became aware how the sounds from the jungle simmered and then died down. No longer did the tiger roar or the monkeys screech. It made him reflect again on the Shan Dragon.

Yente carried on and kept looking. As he neared the temple, something glinted in the long grass off the footpath. He stopped and looked. The Yellow Moonstone. He'd found it. Fantastic. Even as his hand reached to pick it up, he saw it move upwards.

His first impression was how majestic it looked adorning the head of the king cobra which now stared at him with those deadly yellow eyes. Yente backed away. He swallowed hard. He backed away. But still the cobra watched. And followed...along the moonlit path, back, always back to the Shan Temple...

***

Jayna Kan waited in the car a little distance from the Burmese temple. She checked the gold Gucci watch on her wrist and then opened her slim designer handbag. There was little inside the bag. Quickly she found a cigarette and lit it. She drew in the smoke and thought what she must do as she let the smoke escape from her lungs. Jayna glanced again at her watch. Clearly Yente was taking too long to carry out the mission she'd given him.

Another quarter of an hour slipped by and then Jayna left the car. In one hand she held a slim pencil torch in case she needed it. She walked towards the temple, towards the moonlit footpath, quietly, apprehensively. A monkey chattered in the trees ahead of her, somewhere in the jungle a tiger roared but she still continued on her way.

As she walked along the path she felt her skin prickle as if the eyes of the whole world were upon her. She shook off the feeling but knew it still returned.

Her sandals suited the footpath but the skirt with the slit on the side felt a little too tight to her. She'd never walked so far in that particular skirt and certainly not at night in the middle of a jungle. High in the trees something fluttered its wings and she heard a bird screech as it hunted and caught its prey.

The dark peaked outline of the temple loomed ahead of her. Jayna walked steadily towards the entrance. She slipped through the opening offered by the two stone elephants and then allowed herself a few minutes to adjust her eyes to the gloom within the temple. Ahead she saw the carpet of shiny cockroaches. She ignored them and walked on heading for the statue of the Shan Dragon. Quickly she mounted the teak platform and looked for the jewel. She shone her torch to make sure of her discovery. But the jewel wasn't there.

Jayna got down and wondered what had happened. It seemed as if Yente might have stolen the Yellow Moonstone after all. If that was so where was he? She had to find him.

A minute or two later after searching around the statue of the dragon she headed for the exit to the temple. The moon still cast its ghostly light and it seemed even more eerie than before. She looked again but there was no sign of Yente. She started to walk past the two elephants when she tripped. Jayna looked down and wondered what had done that.

Even as she looked something grabbed at her slim ankle and held on. Automatically Jayna screamed and struggled.

In the moonlight she was shocked when she recognised what held her. An arm protruded from under the base of one of the stone elephants. The hand held her ankle. But it hadn't been there when she first entered the temple. The implication escaped her as she tried to think.

She stared at it in horror as she saw the flash of a small ring on one finger. She screamed into the night; she knew it was Yente's ring. It was enough to start her screaming again for a long time.

The jungle animals caught her mood and created a fresh disturbance. The tiger roared and scavenging dogs howled, birds of prey screeched and the elephants trumpeted away. Occasionally monkeys dropped down from the trees to chatter and scared her still further when they leapt up and over her head.

She screamed as she tried to pull away but the grip of the fingers on her ankle proved too much. She screamed once more, a short sharp scream. Then her eyes rolled. After that her screams became one long choking cry of terror.

Unseen by her a figure moved along the footpath dressed in a dark blue robe. The robed figure moved slowly along the footpath until it came up behind Jayna. She still screamed and the monk stood in silence as he withdrew the sword Hanwei from the sheath slung across his broad back. Jayna looked up and screamed, this time only once. In a smooth movement the monk raised and brought the great sword down. A minute or two later his work done the monk wiped the sword on the grass and then with a cotton cloth before returning it to its sheath. Hanwei performed to perfection.

***

Three years later a coach-load of visitors to the Shan Temple remarked on the interesting talk given to them by the tour guide. They fell silent as they entered the Temple of the Shan Dragon.

Soon they stood in a group looking up at the mighty statue above them, on the teak pedestal. The guide pointed out the famous Yellow Moonstone in its collar around the neck of the dragon. There were gasps of appreciation and astonishment at the beauty of the gem.

Then the guide indicated on display a glass case positioned on a table in front of the statue. The case contained the sword Hanwei, and in front of that lay a preserved man's arm.

The inscription, the guide told them, concerned brave Yente who'd lost his arm as he defended the dragon. There followed a reference to the woman Jayna who remained devoted to the shrine. The Burmese guide moved his eyes to the side and the group followed his gaze.

They all saw the grey haired woman sitting cross-legged on a mat in front of the shrine. She looked young but her long hair tied loosely at the neck was pure silver. Only a red flower broke the monotony of her hairstyle. For many hours each day the guide said the woman stayed praying. She would eat only when the kind monks fed her, drink only when they offered her water but always she'd pray. The guide indicated the wooden beads that slipped through her fingers.

An elderly monk standing nearby entered into the conversation.

"And when night time comes we tell Jayna Kan and she gets up. There is no fuss. She leaves behind all that there is of her lover, the hand. He, brave soul, lost it in a fight against thieves trying to steal the Yellow Moonstone, so we honour his courage." The monk pointed to the case. Then he pointed at the back of Jayna. "And so we walk her to the asylum nearby at the end of each day. She has been mad for three years. Harmless but mad.

"There is a mystery surrounding the encounter that fateful night but we ask no questions.

"We can guess, but it is only Jayna who knows what she saw."

Moondust

"Dan Masters made one slip: so, he died and…oops…off came his hand," Adam Garrett said. The Swindon hypnotist looked at his colleague. He paused as he consulted the newspaper cutting taken from the *Oxford Times* on his desk.

"The Masters guy couldn't help being discovered dead, not with a load of cocaine stuffed in his mouth. Now not long after the tip-off, the Thames Valley Police found him with his left hand chopped clean off in the Randolph Hotel, Beaumont Street, Oxford. They recorded it as bizarre, even for the Oxford City Centre and its drugs problems.

"I've done some in depth research and found when a dead man's hand goes missing it is often a hint that dark occult rituals are taking place. It's called the 'dragon's claw', in this area. In Germany it is the 'hand of glory'. Thieves used it to do robberies. I guess I was wrong to think it was all pure myth.

"The strangest thing was the gang responsible for feeding Masters the cocaine didn't hack off his hand. It seems somebody else did that. I'm only drawing this to your attention because there is a link between my one-time patient Robin Abilene and the missing hand. Sure, it is weird, but listen.

"The way I remember it, Robin thought the 'dragon's claw' was made from the hand of a dead man. I laughed, to myself, in disbelief when he told me. He came to see me because of nightmares he had about it. I tried some therapy to get him to forget the object but I had a struggle on my hands. The dreams stayed with him for a long time.

"My recent research after the Randolph Hotel episode showed Robin was quite right to be scared of the strange occult artifact. And I was wrong in what I thought. But when I first saw him as a patient those many months ago I believed what he saw in his dream could have no real foundation. It was pure imagination.

"I guess somehow he knew about the incident in the papers

before it happened and it was important enough to get featured in his dream. I repeat: he mentioned it in his dream. I've got it written down here in my clinical notes. Dreams are dreams. But how could I know Robin was talking about a real occurrence way before it even happened in the Randolph Hotel? That is my puzzle."

For a second Adam's eyes danced over the family photo at the edge of his desk. His wife Barbara smiled at him from the photo, making him remember happier times and almost made him forget the costly divorce facing him. He paused to look across at his colleague Raymond Jackson. Finally his gaze dwelled on the certificate on the office wall awarded to the Swindon Centre of Hypnotherapy. The certificate was enough to focus his mind on the task ahead of him.

"However, I need to talk to you about money," Adam said simply. "Money and my ex-patient Robin Abilene seem to go together so well. The thing about the hand? Well, I got some details off the Internet as well as this newspaper cutting. I'll refer to this point a little later. It is important, strange and demands a good interpretation. It's why I need your help.

"Now, it all depends on moondust, the sort of stuff our kids believe in. For us as adults, I wonder, what will turn myth into reality? I'm sceptical but I'd love moondust to make my wildest dreams come true. This certainly seemed to have happened to Robin. But back to money, or in our case, the lack of it."

Raymond's face went pale as his forehead creased and glistened with sweat. He wriggled on his seat. He slipped a finger inside his shirt collar to loosen the pressure.

"Oh heck. You know about my gambling. It's the same guy you mentioned earlier, Robin Abilene – he covered my debts in the casino. I was stumped to find two thousand pounds and he happened to come along. I did say I'd pay it back, in time. I guess you want to talk about my gambling."

Adam didn't look too shocked at the disclosure. Instead his eyes went to the letter and its contents. Next he cast a glance over the opened manila file on his desk.

"Perhaps, but I really want to chat about money. I've got to lay this on the line: our financial situation is really bad. Your gambling and my divorce are costing us quite a bit."

Raymond coughed and kept his eyes lowered. He blew his nose into a handkerchief.

"Maybe I should have confessed to gambling as my winning

streak seemed to have deserted me. It was lucky Robin turned up and offered to pay my debts. It was an easy option at the time. He recognised my face, and he certainly thinks very highly of you; I knew that from the things he said."

Adam tapped the letter to interrupt his partner.

"But Robin says you've lost over thirty thousand pounds in gambling. He checked with the Casino manager. Is that total right? It does seem a lot to lose. But count yourself lucky bumping into Robin as you did. I've got all the details here in his letter to me. Take a look for yourself."

Adam passed over the letter for Raymond to read.

"I'm not blaming you. I mean I've got problems as well with Barbara, the solicitor and the divorce thing. As if that isn't enough, our company investments have crashed. I'm beginning to get worried how we can go on like this, especially when we got a bad rating with the TV people the last month. The publicity didn't help us at all; we need more people to come to our clinics, not more cancellations." Adam returned to the manila file and extracted a bulky collection of notes and records.

"Our only hope rests on Robin. He seems to favour us. He wants to come and offer us help. I've dug his file out because I need your thoughts on this issue too. Is this moondust at work or have I been dreaming it all? Will you listen and give me your thoughts?"

Raymond's face brightened.

"Sure, I'll help all I can."

Adam Garrett studied the notes again.

"Eighteen months ago Robin came to see me for usual hypnotherapy to sort out voices in his head," Adam began. "These voices kept him awake at night but I resolved the problem in the sessions I had with him. I got him to forget about the voices but not, it seems, the urgency to locate a shop with a blue door in St. John's Wood, London. Once he found the shop his mission was to buy an artifact called the 'dragon's claw'. He said the voices linked good fortune with it.

"Well, I continued with the sessions. I gave him all the usual post hypnotic commands and on one particular session with him we discussed his most recent dream. I thought his dream content dramatic enough without the bizarre way he related everything.

"One day, he didn't turn up. That was the last I heard of him until today, through this letter. Out of interest I dug out this, his file, to check on his past history. I also wanted to tie up some of the things that he claims in his letter. That's why I wanted to confirm with you anything we know about him. To see if he tells the truth, about this gambling urge you have, for instance.

"In a nutshell, Robin was fixated with the inexplicable moondust, the stuff I believed in as a kid and which I'm not too sure about now as I'm a cold discerning sort of guy. Somehow Robin has made moondust his own and he wants to share his good fortune with us. Maybe with his luck our fortunes can be improved."

Adam passed over several stapled sheets of paper extracted from the manila file.

"This is a synopsis of what Robin dreamed about. Now look at the three areas I've highlighted in yellow; those bits are really important. I mean the bit about the 'dragon's claw', the shop with the blue door in St. John's Wood and the man who lost his hand. Those were the three main elements to his dream.

"Here is the chilling stuff. I found a newspaper cutting, with details about the hand incident. I didn't know at the time but it really did take place. Robin was not involved with the killing or the chopped-off hand as he was on holiday in America at the time. It's almost as if he adopted the hand thing into his dream without knowing where he might have gained the information. It is the placing of the incident within his dream that psychologically intrigues me. I swear it is not a coincidence.

"Next the blue door of the shop. I did a search and found the antique shop in St. John's Wood. Out of interest I even went in and spoke to the owner. He remembered selling the 'dragon's claw' to Robin. I found out the claw is a pear woodcarving churned out by a local craftsman. Robin bought it and somehow has stamped his own brand of magic or moondust on it. So, in a fashion, the claw is real. But here, the 'dragon's claw' in the shop is made of wood. In the file on his dream he mentioned about the dead man's hand to be made into a 'dragon's claw'. That was the stuff I suggested to him just did not exist. But do you see how it ties in with the drama in the Randolph Hotel mentioned in the Oxford papers? I'm starting to think everything Robin says is true."

Adam tapped the letter and indicated the address details.

"Now in doing my research I've found out Robin is loaded. His bank manager says he is certainly worth millions. I've checked and he's got a permanent suite at the Hilton Hotel. If we need help I'm sure he will follow through…"

***

"Wow! Some dreams," Raymond commented as he finished reading. "But this 'dragon's claw'?" His gaze kept going back to the sheets of paper he'd just read. "Seems like Robin wanted to find the one described in his dream, but found another in that shop in St. John's Wood instead. How do you see it all fitting in?"

"To me it's a wooden carving, that's all. But in Robin's dream you noticed, I guess, how he gave it the power of witchcraft. He saw it in his dream as being made from a chopped-off hand. Now I know the claw is only a piece of wood but Robin treats it as a tool that makes him money. Isn't that dandy? How he does it? I don't know. He experienced a burning conviction he could do anything with the 'dragon's claw'. Perhaps he can, but something magical has to happen for that to work in his favour. I guess it's safe to say he believed in moondust."

"So, tell me more," said Raymond Jackson.

"He stopped coming to see me, quite abruptly," Adam replied. "He'd always thought I'd done a wonderful job on his head and even said he would give up looking for the 'dragon's claw'. After he left, I never saw him again. Now this is the first contact I've received from him."

"Hang on a minute. If I get this right, Robin stopped looking for the artifact he saw in his dream. I mean the one made from the hand of a dead man?" Raymond interrupted.

"Yes, you've got it. But when he found the shop by accident he said he bought a carving called the 'dragon's claw', and I think he's made it into a special object through his extreme obsession. Robin used his will to seek power, I guess.

"Now in his letter, he mentioned the Bank of Scotland job when sixty-four million pounds went missing. Did I know about it? I do remember the incident blazed across all the newspapers. But what does that bank job have to do with him?"

"Sixty-four million pounds," echoed Raymond sounding as if in a daze.

Adam carried on with his tale.

"As it is, nobody knows exactly how the robbery was carried out.

There is a mystery surrounding it as none of the security staff on duty saw a thing. The time locks on the vaults were in perfect condition and are tamper-proof. The money went missing. Everything the police say is speculation; they don't know.

Now I ask you if by the faintest chance Robin could have stolen the money? If so, tell me how he did it? I've already explained about the 'dragon's claw' being carved wood. If that is so, something magical must have happened to Robin or the 'dragon's claw'. For want of a better word I'm blaming moondust for Robin's find and the fact it worked for him."

"What else does he say in his letter?"

"Well, that he is coming here at eight this evening with a present. But he doesn't say what it is. Could it be the 'dragon's claw'? I'd say no. If something was that good I'm sure he would keep it forever."

"Bet he doesn't turn up," Raymond replied consulting his watch. "He's five minutes late already."

Before Adam could answer, the doorbell rang. The two men looked at each other. It sounded so spooky, in view of what they'd discussed.

"I'll get the door," Raymond volunteered.

Whilst Raymond went to the door, Adam opened a drawer and stared at the needles in a small plastic box. He thought hard. Then he pushed the container out of sight; picked up an automatic pistol. In seconds he slipped it into his pocket. He was ready.

***

Robin's blue eyes sparkled. A big smile brightened his sun-tanned face as he greeted Adam and Raymond. His smart appearance in evening dress impressed both of the hypnotherapists.

"My God, it's good to see you two guys again," Robin enthused as he shook hands. "Lucky I bumped into you the other day, Raymond."

As he finished shaking hands, Robin picked up the two metal suitcases deposited on the floor. He gave one to Adam and the other to Raymond.

"Go on open it," Robin urged. "It's my gift to you for everything you've done for me. It's the very least I can do." He watched as the men flicked open the cases to display the contents. Adam whistled.

"For me? For us?" Adam asked. "How much is there exactly?"

Robin smiled and winked at them.

"Half a million in each case," he said. "I'll drink to that. I guess you will be able to put it to good use?"

The two men nodded. They would have no problem spending the money.

"And you got all this from using the 'dragon's claw' ?" questioned Adam.

Robin smiled again.

"Too true. Thanks for sorting out those voices in my head, Adam. You did a good job there. The claw is exactly like a genie in a bottle to me. It does everything I ask it. If I want money I go to a bank and 'borrow' some. That's what I did to get this stuff for both of you."

"In the papers the bank said the robbery was perfect. Unlike any other in history. Is that true, Robin?" Adam questioned.

Robin nodded; consulted his Rolex wristwatch. He adjusted his black tie and ran a hand over his hair, pushing back a loose strand from his forehead.

"Yes, too true. With the 'dragon's claw' my luck has changed and I love my new lifestyle. I've a house down in the South of France near the resort town of Juan Les Pins. You might care to visit me sometime. Now, look, I must dash, I've got another appointment with a business friend. Bye for now."

In seconds, before the two men could drag their gaze away from the money, Robin disappeared. Yet the door to the office was still firmly shut. Both men shivered expressively.

The second Robin left the building they talked excitedly about his strange exit. It was something that really baffled them. Somehow or other they were starting to believe in moondust, especially when they were each given a case full of money.

For Raymond, money fuelled his love of gambling. To him nothing could compare with the thrill of tossing a coin or spinning a wheel. Always he forgot about the number of times he'd lost. Always he hoped to win more.

Adam too loved money or rather money became his god. Now with the godsend of half a million, Adam hoped to get his divorce and set up home with a certain young woman he'd met at a party. An age difference existed between them but Adam ignored that as he sought more wealth to fan his sexual urges. Greed became his neurosis.

Three minutes later, Adam fired a single shot and got up to take care of a second case full of money with Et-Su marked on the side.

For the first time in his life he felt like a millionaire...

***

Detective Inspector Rod Spinally, called to the scene of the crime, was patient. He addressed the tearful woman in front of him.

"So let's get this quite clear. You came in here and found the two men dead. Raymond Jackson was shot and your husband Adam died because of his insulin swings. Were you aware he'd been warned about his medication in the past?" The Inspector paused and looked at Barbara, Adam's wife. She wiped her eyes with a piece of tissue and sucked in her thin lips.

"That's right," Barbara confirmed. "The doctors kept telling him but he said he knew best. Sometimes he'd miss an injection completely."

"I know we were going to get a divorce but all the same for this to happen right now is not at the best of times. Sure we have no children but there are other issues like the will, the house and what happens next. I'm on my own now, on this one."

The DI nodded and made another note on the sheet in front of him.

"Was your late husband a careless man?"

Barbara shook her head and blew her nose. She sniffed.

"I didn't know about that," she admitted, "but he has always got fed up with medical matters in the past. His nature, I guess."

The DI nodded and drew the interview to a close. He got a form printed for a signature and when it was completed he saw Mrs Garrett leave the building.

After she'd left, he went through the footage of the video camera. On the first camera the only piece of interest was the clip showing Raymond Jackson at about 8 o'clock opening the door to a client. Whoever was at the door did not register on the TV screen and neither was there evidence of anybody entering the building. Yet further footage showed Jackson walking along the corridors, talking away yet being completely alone. The DI admitted to his superiors at a later date how puzzled he was at the time.

It was nagging doubt regarding what really happened that made the DI look at the second and third CCTV camera tapes on the business site.

***

When Barbara found the bodies of the two dead men she also saw the two cases. One look at the money was enough to set her off. Her eyes glinted with greed as she realised the money was there for the taking. It was true she called Wiltshire Constabulary but only after the act of removing the cases. She placed the money in the boot of her car.

Now the interview was over, Barbara felt she could relax. Her bright blue Honda handled like a dream but maybe it was taking the money home with her that put the big smile on her face.

***

It was after midnight when Barbara awoke. She turned on the table light and wondered what was happening. She stayed in bed trying to puzzle out the strange feeling within her body. The door to the bedroom was open. On hearing her move, her black Labrador entered the room, demanding attention. Barbara leant across and scratched the dog's ears.

Another sound caught her notice. She looked up to see the door of the bedroom open slightly wider. Next it opened wider still and her dog now stared at something in silence.

Barbara swallowed hard and drew the covers up around her neck. She watched with bated breath as the door to the bedroom creaked and something came into the room. It was the way in which the dog reacted that got her. First the dog looked up – up at the something, with its tail still for once. Then it looked down without barking. She felt spooked by the event and by the inexplicable behaviour of her guard dog.

Moments later when the mood passed, she opened the door to the cupboard. Before she even looked to check on the cases containing the money, she knew they were gone.

All that remained was a strange white powder on the floor. She rubbed it with her fingers and tried smelling it. It had no smell. But by rights how could there be when she didn't believe in moondust? And neither did the Wiltshire Police who came to knock on her door later on the same day.

***

The church in the tiny village of Little Coxwell had developed a leaky roof. It wasn't really surprising, since the quaint church built in Norman times was overdue for repair and renovation.

As Rector Jim Crockett contemplated, it was only the lack of funds that was stopping him from calling in the builders. There was also the question of the wooden pews being eaten away by death-watch beetles. As he sat there, praying with his eyes shut, he couldn't help but wonder how he could solve his money problems. Unexpectedly it started to rain inside the church. The whisper, the rustlings were the first signs he heard, until he felt the 'waves' break, as if he were on a beach.

The rector opened his eyes and jumped to his feet in amazement. He didn't believe what he was seeing.

"Praise the Lord," the rector shouted. "Praise the Lord," he shouted again with his face tilted upwards.

It was impossible to disguise his excitement. His face was shining as he held out his arms, snatching in ecstatic delight at the banknotes drifting down all around him. Even as he watched, more money poured down. It made him run around as if berserk, stuffing the money into piles of black bags.

He shouted when the sexton appeared and together they continued collecting the money, which appeared in answer to his frenzied prayer. The whole incident appeared to be miraculous.

"Without counting," the sexton said, "you've got a gold mine here."

Rector Jim Crockett nodded. "Too true. The Lord moves in mysterious ways. He has answered my prayers. Now we can get the roof and those other things all sorted out. What a day! Thank you Lord. Thank you Lord."

The rector and the sexton knelt down in the church to offer their own prayers to God for the 'bread' from Heaven. They closed their eyes and gave thanks to a powerful God.

***

Detective Inspector Rod Spinally, of Wiltshire Police, faced the woman in the interview room. He stared deep into her eyes and set the tape recorder going. Alongside the DI, a woman constable sat taking notes.

"Now, Mrs Barbara Garrett, when we ran the CCTV tape yesterday we came across an interesting piece of footage. It was on the camera in the office car park. Why don't you own up and tell us what happened. You could save us all a lot of time."

The DI got up and pressed a switch. Immediately the video recorder came on, and on the TV screen Barbara again saw herself loading two metal cases into the boot of her car.

A moment later the DI froze the frame.

"See that there – those letters on the cases. It spells out the word Et-Su. It might not mean much to you but a million pounds was stolen in cases with that code on the outside. The money disappeared from the Bank of Scotland in Oxford City. We can see you handled the cases, so we know you must have the money. Well?"

Mrs Barbara Garrett buried her face in her hands. She knew she was really up against an impossible situation. Who was going to believe her story? She could admit to loading the cases of money into her car but since then they had literally disappeared from her home. And what about the dead men?

"I don't know," she managed to get out. The DI's face hardened. He clicked with his tongue and shook his head. A gasp, a sob left Barbara's throat.

Now nobody would believe her story. The only thing to convince anybody would be moondust. But first she'd have to believe in it herself.

And for Barbara, that was the 'rub.'

The Sealed Envelope

The black severed dragon claw lay on the table in the hall. Everything about it hinted at evil.

As my visitor went past it, I saw his face grimace with horror: he was impressed. His eyes flickered over the dried bats' corpses pinned to the white walls and the mass of cobwebs hanging from a corner of a doorway. Black netting covered an easy chair, and over it crawled shiny snakes.

I guess people can read all they want to about dragon magic but Tim Wilkins was desperate for a firm demonstration, and I could give him one at a price, of course.

I led the way into the dimly-lit study where all my work was done. Again I saw Wilkins's eyes casting about, taking in the grinning skulls set high on a bookcase behind me. He sniffed the air. The incense made him cough. I noticed beads of sweat on his face and hands. He was scared but he was here tonight.

"So, how can I help you? My fee for hexing is fifteen hundred pounds, Mr..." I left him in no doubt with my Cockney accent where I was born. He blinked and his eyes took in my receding forehead and those tufts of hair that hung down on each side just above my ears.

"Tim...er...Tim Wilkins. I can pay - I've the money here...in old notes, as your friend said. It's my boss I want dead...Can you do it?"

I checked the notes and then put them away.

"Of course...I need his name."

Wilkins nodded and then took out a sealed envelope from his pocket. His face was white as he laid it on the table and tapped it with his finger. I could tell he was scared, by the way his eyes scarcely shifted their gaze from the sealed envelope.

I couldn't help but wonder whose name was inside the envelope.

"It's here."

His pencil-thin lips trembled as he kept staring at the envelope.

"Good. I'll start tonight. With the 'Black Candle of Death' your boss will die inside a week. Rely on me. This is real dragon magic."

Wilkins seemed satisfied and glad I didn't request the name of the victim outright. Minutes later when he left, I kissed the dragon's claw and shouted. I was pleased no end.

***

"Penny."

A shapely blonde wiggled out of the kitchen. As she click-clacked her way towards me, she was smiling and holding a broomstick in one hand, a rubber snake in the other. I knocked them out of the way as I grabbed her. My mouth found her soft red lips. Hmm. I kissed her again. Fun and delight. I couldn't stop talking as I took off the half-wig and latex mask. I was amazed at how quickly the mask had transformed my neat hairline into a balding patch. Then with the tufts of hair on the side of my head from the half-wig, it was no wonder Tim Wilkins failed to recognise me. I reflected on my accent which had helped the deception along even further. I carried on thinking about my successful acting as I removed the grease paint. A final wipe with a tissue and I faced Penny with a smile on my face.

"Clever little Rock Anderson, aren't you?" Penny cooed. She straightened the thin straps of her little black dress. "Wilkins was in the pub last night...didn't he recognise you at all, Rock?" I thought it funny as she slipped into a Cockney accent to match the one I'd used on Tim Wilkins. But we both enjoyed acting all the time.

I shook my head and took the money from her.

"For fifteen hundred pounds he must want somebody to die very badly indeed. Poor sucker. Whatever his name is!" She sighed as she looked at the sealed envelope.

When I met Wilkins in the Crown pub in Faringdon's Market Place he moaned about being a bank clerk, and let slip he'd do anything to get rid of his troublesome boss. I wasn't too worried about him working hard. I was more interested in harvesting some money as an idea popped into my head.

You see, acting is my chosen career, though at the moment I'm 'resting' between engagements. Now lucky for me Lucinda Cooper purchased a large quantity of black magic props from an old junk shop in Camden, London. She was already thinking about future theatre productions and we helped by looking after the props. My girlfriend

Penny aided in the deception by laying out the necessary items before naïve Tim Wilkins called with the sealed envelope.

I knew I was on a winning streak because if he went to Thames Valley Police how could he admit he paid me to kill his boss by hexing? Also he never saw through my disguise - even though we held a conversation in the pub last night. But to be perfectly fair, I'm an expert at voices, so how could my barrow-boy patter not deceive him? Tomorrow Penny and I would start a new season in Cornwall.

We celebrated our good luck by opening a bottle of whisky after we packed away some of the black magic items into a large wicker basket. It was ready to be loaded into the car tomorrow morning.

Later, the same night when Penny went to bed and I drank enough whisky to get sober again, I picked up the book on dragon magic that came with the stage props. I started to read.

***

On the table in front of me lay the sealed envelope from Wilkins. I resisted the temptation to open it. I did resolve, however, to try out a 'Black Candle' to see if this 'dragon magic' worked, and maybe to give Tim Wilkins a little of his money's worth.

The room was dark as I struck a match and lit the black candle. It cast an eerie yellow light about the room and made the furniture leap into terrifying shapes and shadows.

The only audible sound in the room was the ticking of the grandfather clock. *Tick. Tock. Tick…* I sensed a change of atmosphere…but perhaps it was my imagination. My glance flickered for a second on the grinning skulls above my head on the bookcase.

I slid the sealed envelope under the burning candle. What I did next was without reason but then I love a bit of fun. I picked up a pen and pulled out the envelope from underneath the black candle. Very carefully I wrote the name 'Tim Wilkins' on the outside of it. Then I slid the sealed envelope back to start the ritual. A moment later I said the magic dragon words of 'KAMM KARANA CUM NAVAJ OTTO BEACORA FINABUS', as stated in the book. I sat in silence as the seven minutes ticked away. The beat of the clock sounded so loud in my ears. *Tick. Tock.* At the end of the allotted time I blew out the candle and went to bed. Penny was asleep, wrapped up in her own dreams.

The next morning I began packing the cases when the phone

rang. It was Tim Wilkins. He sounded very distressed.

"Forget it - what I asked you to do. I've changed my mind."

"Hang on a minute, Mr Wilkins. What's wrong? You sound terrible and what about the money?"

"I'm scared...the strange dream I experienced last night upset me...look, give me my money back...it's not mine...I borrowed it," Wilkins said. I could tell he was going to pieces.

"Tough," I said as I slammed the receiver down. I went and found Penny to explain what was happening.

"Come on, Penny, let's get out of here fast," I said. Well, we tried to leave but the flat tyre on the car needed to be fixed. As I struggled to change the wheel, we heard a deafening crash from around the corner. Penny ran down the road to see what it was. I found out soon enough...When she returned I saw her face was serious, unsmiling. Unconsciously she was dry washing her hands. Something terrible had spooked her. Behind her lumbered a police constable who introduced himself. He wanted to talk to me.

"Need your help, sir," the constable explained. "There's been an accident and one of the two chaps who got killed carried your name and this address on a bit of paper. We found it in his hand when he died. There are other names on the same bit of paper, but as you happened to be so close I thought I'd pop along for a chat. I'll talk to all the other people on the list eventually."

As an actor I recognised the old policeman's quaint Wiltshire accent. He was large, obviously waiting for retirement I guessed by his age and grey hair. Now it appeared he was in charge of an accident and needed my assistance in some way.

I agreed to go along and help but more unsettling news was to come. He told me witnesses claimed the Fiat was lifted and hurled over a four-foot wall straight into the sitting room of a nearby house. The driver and passenger died instantaneously. It was weird and frightening. I was stunned by the constable's words. Surely I couldn't be to blame for what happened? In my head I could hear the grandfather clock ticking away. *Tick. Tock. Stop. Clock.* I shuddered. Must get a grip on myself.

My sympathetic face went on. It was easy, remember I'm an actor. I decided to play it cool. There was nothing to link me with the fifteen hundred pounds I'd taken off Wilkins. It was pure bad luck he happened to have my name and address on him when he died. However, in spite of my efforts at deception, I guess the astonishment showed on my face when the constable informed me of the names of the two dead men.

"The younger man was Tim Wilkins and he was with his boss Archie Napier. It is a very common name, I know. Anything wrong?"

"No," I lied and got away as quick as I could. I was scared because my real name was Archie Napier before I became an actor; now I am known as Rock Anderson.

Maybe my stab at dragon magic worked with a vengeance. But to me it was soon obvious I was venturing into the occult areas I knew very little about.

I was worried by the car flying over the four-foot wall and remembered something in the book of magic I'd half read...about the summoning up of dragons. So with trembling fingers I turned the pages and saw my foolish error. By mistake I had concocted two spells into one...I let the book slip from my grasp...now I ripped the outside of the sealed envelope.

I gasped at the name - my real name and staggered outside to tell Penny...it was then that I had a heart attack. I closed my eyes as the pain increased.

***

Somebody mentioned the Great Western Hospital, Swindon, and I awoke hours later to find myself rigged up to various machines. It was dark...night time…though I was suffering, something nagged away inside my brain. A nurse came and went away. Then…I heard a noise...a peculiar chuckle...but nobody was there in the room. I raised my head and tried looking around.

At first I saw nothing...next came the two tiny red eyes blazing out of a small dark form with wings shimmering down its back. I was petrified as it moved out from the dark corner and started to pull out the wires connecting me to the life saving machines...again the chuckle...then the beastly roar and a blast of hot air as flames shot towards me...

In that fraction of a second I knew Rock Anderson would never have his name in lights in the West End - but it would look quite good on an impressive gravestone.

Merlin's Grimoire

The man was tall, about 7 feet 6 inches tall, I guessed. As I sat on the park bench and looked at him I felt intimidated by his height. I also guessed he was some five stones heavier than my mere twelve stone weight.

My legs jellied as he hunched his broad shoulders and looked down at me, Gary Preston. His grip of high-tensile steel on my scrawny arms drew me closer to his face. I suffered in silence as every inch of getting nearer meant a real notch of terror.

In his Jesuit habit he looked so fierce, so foreboding, his bloodshot eyes staring out of sockets like sunken wells. I saw his yellow-hued skin drawn drum-tight across the bones of his face. There was something very disturbing about such a big man.

His shaven head, like a Buddhist priest, glistened with sweat. On his large hands, the backs covered with bushy black hairs, were the strangest tattoo marks. I noticed on one finger he sported a glittering ruby ring. Here was a blast from the past, a man to fear.

My visit to the BBC Antiques Roadshow in Faringdon the day before never prepared me for such a shock. The sight of this strange giant of a man was enough to make me shiver. I was so glad my girlfriend Linda had not come with me to the meeting place in the local park.

"Gary Preston. You have the paper?" the man croaked in a rasping voice. He held out his hands and shook them impatiently. I half expected him to produce a knife and cut my throat. "Show me, minnow. Now!"

I took the shoebox out of the carrier bag. I fumbled, then pushed off the lid to display the bit of paper responsible for his erratic behaviour. What a fuss for a small scrap of paper. Or was there latent power behind the words written on the innocent looking note? I was being paid well, so I guess I really didn't need to know.

"Ah. Yes. Yes. Sweet Merlin. Wonderful magician Merlin." The man smiled and punched the air with delight. "Good work, Gary."

He took the shoebox and from his roomy habit he drew out a small brown parcel. He tore open the edge; passed it to me. I knew immediately what I saw; the twenty-pound notes were only too familiar to me.

"Money. It's all there. Check, ye of little faith." His strange way of speaking puzzled me. I wondered about the man but with hindsight on your side you can be an expert at anything, even astro-physics.

"No problem. Okay," I returned, taking the money and fanning through the notes. "I trust you…Mister…?"

"Rodac. Black Rodac. I am the servant of Merlin," the man said. I started to feel more confident now I'd got Black Rodac talking.

"Oh, I know of Merlin. Everybody loves King Arthur. But is there more money, where you come from? I'm interested," I said. "Maybe we could deal."

"Deal? Dream again, Gary. I who am Merlin's Vanguard, I from the Shadowland of Amaraga, I who must now return there," Black Rodac said.

"Seems a waste," I said. "You obviously got forgotten by our Merlin. Seems like you know a lot, especially where there is lots of money."

First there came a grunt, followed by Black Rodac shifting his position. He glanced around, his frightening eyes directed at all the people walking through the park. Innocent people paused. Some teenagers blinked at him in surprise; looked away. A moment later he was off, his boat-like feet pounding the tarmac pathway as he powered his way through the crowd of tourists. Large gaps opened up for him, so soon he was lost to my view.

***

The BBC Antiques Roadshow in Faringdon had seemed to cast a hypnotic spell over me. Though a criminal, I was proud of my English heritage. Old worthies like King Arthur, Merlin and St. George meant a lot to me. But I'd have liked it better if I'd found the Holy Grail. Guess I could have sold it for a vast fortune.

I knew people liked old historic things; they enjoyed antiques and I was keen to see what rich people visited the Antiques Roadshow. Linda couldn't understand my interest until I mentioned ripe wallets ready for stealing.

As I watched the antiques experts at work, I couldn't help but notice an old woman struggle into the Leisure Centre with a carrier bag in each hand. She looked about sixty, with long grey hair tied in a bun. Her low-heeled shoes were well-worn, and the bright red scarf around her neck contrasted with her green waxed jacket. I kept a quiet eye on her out of curiosity as she approached her appraiser. It seemed a long time before he managed to inspect her items.

The silver-tongued expert picked up the pewter tankard she'd pulled out of the shopping bag. He faced the roving BBC camera.

"Mrs Kennedy, it's quite superb, worth about three thousand pounds," he said. His fingers traced out the fine engravings on the tankard. He clearly loved the article. The old woman sighed with surprise at his valuation. He put the article down and moved on.

Excitedly his eyes lit up as he noticed a dusty book with the word 'Merlin' on the spine. Mrs Kennedy laid it carefully on the table. I watched the expert as he turned his attention to the book. The way he treated it interested me. Clearly there was something the appraiser knew and I didn't.

"Can this be Merlin's *Grimoire*?" His question was to the camera as it moved in closer.

He blew off the layer of dust and opened the book gingerly. He started to read.

"Priceless - but it cannot be the real McCoy." He went quiet as he concentrated on the page before him.

Before Mrs Kennedy could answer, a flash of lightning zipped through the hall, followed by a swirling purple cloud. It was this that enveloped him completely.

The audience gasped with disbelief at the bizarre occurrence. I also gasped. I swallowed hard too. I sensed the raw electricity in the air; almost as if 'something' esoteric had been set in train. Instinctively, I knew more was to come. I shivered, perhaps with excitement, or the sudden coldness of the hall.

Soon the purple fog cleared but though I looked, I could see no sign of the expert. Yet I swear I could still hear him talking, his voice coming out of the air or ether. Was I really a witness to something so weird?

Every person present in the hall gravitated towards Merlin's *Grimoire*. Its interest value far outshone the gothic and the Victorian paraphernalia found in any show. Those nearest shuffled forward for a better look. The *Grimoire* lay open on the table, its yellowed parchment-like pages marked with a black ribbon.

"Invisibility spell," a woman exclaimed. "Well I'll be damned."

It was true, a man had disappeared, with the hint of more sinister happenings to follow. Already I heard the familiar sound -- the police sirens approaching at high speed.

I felt the tension, the excitement, and the adrenaline flowing as I made my move. With the single-mindedness of a coiled cobra I stole a couple of wallets and managed to leave before the police arrived.

But before I left, I picked up a small scrap of paper I had seen drift out of the *Grimoire* and land on the floor.

Later the same evening as I watched BBC television I remembered the paper. I took it out and read 'Secara Amagara Faboraca'. Some strange language, but its meaning was lost on me. I never did Latin or foreign languages at the approved school. I wondered about throwing it away.

The land phone came alive. Linda was combing her long blonde hair when it rang. "For you, Gary. Some strange guy."

"Merlin's *Grimoire* has gone, but I need the paper you picked up today, Gary Preston," the croaky-voiced man said. "I can pay; no problem there. Shall we settle on seven thousand pounds?"

I was flabbergasted, but still an opportunist.

"Make it seven and a half thousand."

"Don't get greedy. I know all about you, Gary. Tell me, how is your friend Angelo? He used to be quite good looking. He was such a one for the women. The police are making connections. Seems he doesn't say much these days. Somebody didn't like him, 'alive', should I say. Now wise up, bring the paper and we can exchange.

"One last thing. Those two wallets you stole. Do what I say and you'll find you won't get caught. OK?"

***

I sat on the teak bench in the park, my thoughts churning away with seven thousand pounds in my pocket. I shuddered when I thought of the man to whom I'd given the piece of paper. A thought suddenly struck me. I remembered my blonde darling Linda. I used my mobile to text her. I decided we were going to holiday in Madrid tomorrow morning.

I had scarcely put the mobile away when I felt the snap of

handcuffs on my wrists. I looked up into a familiar face. Not again.

"Better come along with us," Detective Inspector Tony Ripon said. "We've got you Hollywood-style on film. Let's pop down to the station, shall we? Them BBC boys did some good filming yesterday, so we know you were there when it happened."

Three hours later I was sick of the questions but glad the police hadn't got anything out of me. I was wise; I knew my rights.

"Look, on the video you can see yourself in the hall. So why not come clean and tell us what you've been up to," the DI cajoled. "Make it easy for us all."

The BBC had passed footage to the police, which placed me in the audience of the Faringdon Antiques Roadshow. As I watched, a sudden testing thought struck me. What had I got to lose? I remembered what the man had said.

"I stole two wallets," I admitted. There was mock regret on my face.

"Nonsense, nobody reported any stolen. Mind you a staff member of the road show disappeared. Also did you know the old girl Dorothy Kennedy died of a heart attack? Who was the man in the park? What about cocaine and your dealer friend Angelo? Tell us about the seven thousand pounds we found on you."

So the strange man was right; no wallets were reported as stolen.

After a short break, the DI strutted back into the room. He waved photographs at me. He wore a supercilious smile.

"Gary, look at these photos taken of your rendezvous in the park with Mr Big. Who is he? I know it's not Angelo: lead poisoning finished him off in the Bristol docks.

"Do you know we recently had a sighting of your Mr Big?" The DI scanned my face for any trace of emotion, anything that might give the game away. But I wasn't saying much and deliberately kept my thoughts to myself.

Mind you, his information on good old Angelo interested me. Now I knew for sure he was dead. I was now puzzling out how Mr Big could have known in advance Angelo had been shot. It sort of worried me.

The DI spread the photographs across the table.

"Look at this one." The DI stopped quite abruptly. "What the hell? It's too strange. Get Dirk down here, and his brains. I want to know what's gone wrong. Now!"

I watched in fascination and some amusement as the DI flicked through the pile of photographs. Even from where I sat, it was evident I was the only person captured on film. I recognised the location in the park from the teak bench and myself on film.

I sat on the bench. SNAP. A packet of money hovered in mid air. SNAP. Money in my hand. SNAP. But no police photographic record existed of the inexplicably strange tall man.

Then I noticed my shadow on the ground and, it beggars belief, to my horror a second larger shadow as if cast by a giant…

The interview dragged on but I knew if I kept my cool I could get to keep the money. In fact the DI wanted to talk to me about it before letting me go home.

He placed the packet of money on the desk in front of me and looked me in the face.

"There's the money we took off you."

I couldn't help grinning. Maybe now my luck was changing.

"However, to find out we had to check every note. Every single note. They were all clean, except one pack of twenty-pound notes used as part payment to Angelo for drugs.

"We think Angelo's murderer stole the money after killing him, without being aware we planted it in an undercover operation. Now with Angelo dead I'm wondering how on earth you got hold of the notes. But if you killed him you'd certainly know, so how about telling us? Or are you still going to blame Mr Big?"

Remains

The alien child Sycy gripped the hand of the elder firmly. Her body trembled as the glowing planet they sought came into view. The sound of the pulsar engines hummed in a higher note inside their spacecraft yet failed to distract her gaze from Earth: the planet of death.

"Tell me, Grandfather, tell me again why my parents died and how I was rescued? What is so deadly about TETRA energy bursts? Tell me everything, Grandfather. Everything."

The elder alien studied the glowing planet and then the face of his grandchild, Sycy. He noted the blemishes, the tiny holes created on her facial skin surface by the radiation pulses from Earth. Then he started to relate how it all began and what led to the ultimate disaster...

***

With wide, frightened eyes, the lonely Roman auxiliary watched the white light cross the dark night sky.

The absent stars and the dim moon contrasted against the bright pulsating light as it zipped across the heavens on some predetermined course. The sentry froze at his vantage point, a sub-fort on the enormous length of Hadrian's Wall. He knew fellow soldiers also watched the night sky but he still felt alone. He tightly gripped his spear, confirmed his *gladius* was ready for use in its sheath as prayers to his god tripped over his lips. At that point he wished himself at home with his family.

The white light stopped and hovered before it plummeted to the ground. The watching soldier on the Roman wall estimated it fell over a thousand paces away. Immediately he thought of brigands and attacks by local rebels.

Barely had that white light disappeared than yellow light flickered into life to his left; the first feeble flames quickly transformed into a brightly burning beacon as dry kindling caught fire to drive the flames up some twelve feet. The beacon was lit by his fellow campaigners camped in a settlement on top of a nearby hill. Presumably, on seeing that strange white light, they made known something out of the ordinary was happening. In answer hundreds of other beacons burst into life. Each beacon of yellow light meant a cluster of men along the famous Hadrian's Wall. Besides sending out warnings, the light and warmth from his thoughtful comrades at the manned outposts cheered him up.

Eventually all the signal-beacons along Hadrian's Wall burned out; in contrast, the night seemed even blacker. It left the auxiliary alone with his fears and thoughts once more. As he paced his section of the stone wall on regular patrols, he thought about the old woman suspected of witchcraft. The previous day many accused her of poisoning a child and using her power to summon up evil spirits. At her execution on Hadrian's Wall, she spat out a curse which invoked all manners of evil things from the depth of Hades.

Perhaps the strange white light was connected somehow with the curse? Maybe it was the devil lurking on the horizon? Could this be a call for sacrifice? The more the auxiliary thought about it, the more frightened he became. All through the long night his eyes hardly ever strayed far from where he'd seen the white light.

Many hours later, as dawn lightened the area, he noticed a torch light some distance off. Sweat soaked his tunic when this light came closer: in terror he remembered the legionaries who had gone off to find local resistance groups. These soldiers attacked the nearby village of Penbury to show off the strength of the Roman army. The skirmish between Penbury was an old one as the village always harboured rebels, so they deserved to be punished. Closer still came the yellow flickering torchlight, and very soon the approaching soldiers would cross the field where the strange white light had disappeared. The auxiliary felt fearful; his forehead creased as he peered into the night. The minutes ticked away, generating more tension inside his body.

Again, he fingered the token hung on a rough cord around his neck. Once more he prayed for his fellow soldiers. Without warning, the bright white light pulsated through the trees and concentrated in the same area as the marching legionaries. It hunted them.

A great shout went up. He heard men scream, then yell out in terror as the white light rose high into the night sky. In seconds it was absorbed by a larger blob of light that disappeared without trace. Darkness fell again, leaving the auxiliary alone with his fears.

But though the night was completely black, he heard noises. Hadrian's Wall generated a hive of activity because of the white light. Men shouted across from one sentry post to another. The auxiliary heard drums pound away and horns blast out warnings. More torches sprang into life. Shallow trenches of oil flared up providing more illumination. Torches fixed on the ends of spears cast further light. In the fields, horses and cattle milled around in panic. A strong wind carried sparks and embers enough to set a mound of fodder alight. All those incidents added to the confusion felt by the auxiliary that night.

The beacons and drums helped provide some reassurance but nobody knew exactly what was happening. Hadrian's Wall snaked away for miles right in front of the auxiliary. And not too far away from him, near an entrance, he heard a great disturbance. The auxiliary, unable to leave his post, learned by shouting to others about the soldier returning from Penbury who'd staggered in. It seemed he and fellow soldiers encountered a bright white light cast by strange creatures. The alien beings rendered them all unconscious but this man came to first and his shouts immediately drew medical assistance from the Roman Army.

***

The man told his story in a few words; he thought strange creatures attacked, unlike any other known being. His colourful description terrified all those in the fort who remembered myths, legends and the use of witchcraft.

Shortly, soldiers returned to the fort carrying ten men on stretchers. These ten men suffered from shock, the victims of the mysterious attack. It was also discovered that a missing soldier, Sitanius, was thought by some to have been kidnapped by the aliens, perhaps to appease the gods...

Once named, the missing soldier caused endless speculation. Sitanius, a relative to a distant cousin of the Roman Senator Veronious Vega, was never seen again. But the soldiers who had lived and fought alongside the tough Roman soldier made him famous: they employed a mason to carve pictures on a stone slab.

The slab showed brave Sitanius sucked up into the sky by a winged creature encircled by rays of light. On the ground danced the stricken matchstick men; in the background the instantly recognizable Hadrian's Wall equipped with a burning beacon.

***

Excavations of Hadrian's Wall over 2,000 years later revealed the stone slab and a clay bust of Sitanius. This find proved important, for it offered a clue to what Sitanius looked like and what occurred on the stone barrier, near Penbury, when alien creatures attacked.

As the excavation progressed, members of a local running club, the Penbury Pounders, found themselves chased by a man dressed in an authentic-looking Roman uniform. He even carried a *gladius*. Though slowed down by full uniform and sandals he seemed determined to catch the runners. The Pounders joked about the situation; they all thought it a stunt on historical Hadrian's Wall.

Unfortunately, their laughter dried up when the man stabbed the last two runners with his sword. Terror filled the others as he chased them. More runners received wounds before the rest scattered across the fields to escape the crazy killer.

The police arrived to search the surrounding countryside but the 'Roman' had gone. At a nearby farm, however, the watchdog had its throat and belly cut.

Days later, Val Barton, a junior school art teacher, gave a chilling account of the two Roman soldiers who tried running towards her car while shouting and waving their swords. Quickly she accelerated away and reported to the police.

"Here's my sketch of the two men. They look alike, like twins. Both dressed in Roman uniform and carrying swords. See for yourself, Inspector."

The Detective Inspector visited the scene of the crime. He made an interesting discovery.

"No sign of them Romans, but what's this, Constable? A coin. A Roman coin and in mint condition too. I reckon something strange is going on. Get this checked out."

Routine carbon dating tests at Harwell, Didcot, showed the coin to be as old as Rome itself. The police postulation was limited: they thought the coin was a replica, the uniform a theatrical prop and the killer some psycho. A complete lack of motive for the killings caused their theory to flounder.

As the months slipped by, the attacks increased, as did the

number of men involved. On every occasion, eyewitnesses claimed the men, whether two, three or four, looked identical in every detail. This fact became evident in a lucky photograph taken by a witness using a digital camera. Such evidence supported the sketch provided by art teacher Val Barton.

The public, following the Roman incident in the press and mass media, considered the government and police laggardly when it came to solving the riddle of the 'Roman Ripper' as the press dubbed him/them. But, though the police failed to make an arrest, behind the scenes all available information was being gathered concerning the Roman killers.

The local police and three other forces pooled their information on the 'Roman Ripper'. The files became bigger as even more information reflected press cuttings and information from around the world. Even as the public worried endlessly, the Home Secretary employed specialists to work closely with the struggling police force.

John Tudor, an American investigator concerned with national security, and Arthur Booker, his British counterpart, attempted to solve the riddle. The two met in Penbury. Each man carried a file with data pertinent to the strange phenomena. The data was wide-ranging; they even linked a radiation pulse in space with the timing of each Roman sighting. It seemed that whenever the TETRA radiation increased a Roman appeared. Both men pondered that thought...

Through various sources they learned of the capture of a Roman soldier by the Russians. A spy penetrated the Kola complex, a massive weapons establishment, at the same time as a UFO was sighted. The clandestine report revealed the spy was captured wearing a Roman uniform and though tortured by the KGB, he never confessed to anything. The soldier's fate was a mystery. Though it was assumed they killed him, one report said his body evaporated. As the KGB blamed the West it was important to find out the identity of the mysterious intruder.

***

"John, everything about this case sounds incredible. I'm thinking about the sketches we have and the Identikit drawings. They all relate to the same man. Because of the sightings, often simultaneous but miles apart, we know it can't be possible. All I can say this appears to be a legacy of some sort, something that has its roots in the past."

"My file reflects all the information gathered by the British security services and the police, plus I've made notes as well. Look at the photograph, the sketch of the Roman soldier and look at the CC footage. Can it be a shot of the same person?" Arthur paused to point at the pictures in his open file. He then continued to speak.

"Most attacks have been on or near Hadrian's Wall. Do we make that our first clue? Now consider the stone slab and the clay bust of Sitanius. Not forgetting that Val Barton identified his ugly face. I'm guessing Sitanius is our man, perhaps even our killer." Arthur Booker frowned as he thought about the problem.

"Maybe he is. But why should Sitanius haunt us?" John Tudor said.

"Who knows? Perhaps Sitanius got kidnapped and then what? I'm thinking there is some master plan here."

"But what's gone wrong to bring about the return of these soldiers hundreds of years after they were taken?" John Tudor replied.

"Who knows? It's not only Britain; it's happening all around the world. I guess it's all to do with time. Is time flexible like this bit of string for instance?" Arthur Booker held up the piece of string he'd been playing with. "Keep thinking about time and maybe we might get somewhere. I really feel something went wrong in those Roman Britain days."

John listened and shuddered expressively. He poured whisky into two tumblers and pushed one towards Booker. It was late evening and they'd been talking and comparing notes for many hours. It had been a full, tiring day.

The radio was on and they both heard the news broadcast from the Space Agency in Florida, USA.

"A supremo-class Russian spaceship today went off course and collided with the latest Eros satellite jointly owned by a European consortium. Apart from the financial aspects of this, the first major accident in space…the many years of work lost to the space research program...few can disagree more core safety is needed...a complete check on space routes, inter-space undertaking...and the new type of TETRA vibrations following the accident. TETRA radiation is a new killer..." The startling news droned on.

Now as Arthur looked up at the dark sky through the open window of the rooming house, he thought about John's words. It was too incredible. But could there be a grain of truth in what they discussed tonight? He went cold as a white light spread out from one end of the sky to the other. He thought about dragon-ships. "Oh, my God," Arthur exclaimed. "John. What we dreaded...Is this it?"

From the white stream of light covering the sky came more concentrated buttons of light. They zipped away and sped towards the earth. They could see tens of thousands of them, and as some touched the ground nearby, soldiers in Roman battle-dress appeared. More and more landed, and they watched in fascination as the Romans arranged themselves into legion formation. And the legions started to march.

Still more buttons of white light came out of the night sky and more soldiers arrived. There seemed to be no end to their numbers. Soon, an army passed their house and everywhere they looked seemed thick with Roman soldiers. In the distance stood Hadrian's Wall. The lights moving along the pathway on the wall showed it to be covered with soldiers. Even as they watched, beacons spotted the surrounding countryside guiding the soldiers in the dark on to different locations. Adding to the mayhem caused by the Roman lights and torches, the security services released rockets and warning flares. From overhead jets screamed and helicopters beat their own rhythm. From all around the muffled sounds of horns seemed to pull the soldiers into a coherent army. The heavy drums joined the horns and then came the silver sound of trumpets. Men shouted and yelled adding to the extravaganza of noise and confusion.

John and Arthur watched the superb Roman fighting machine head onto fixed destinations. Was Penbury the only place where the Roman soldiers had landed? Arthur phoned his MI5 boss in London: no, they were everywhere, it seemed - in the background he could hear gunshots...Branden told him:

"The army have tried all sorts of ways to stop them but still they keep coming - there must be millions of them! The sky's full...They come in on some sort of blue bubble that bursts as it touches the ground and out jumps another bloody Roman! Kill one and he only vaporizes, to be replaced by a dozen more. We can fight and - "

The line went dead; a vital link with the rest of the world was severed.

Then they heard a noise at the back of their house: the wooden gate was forced open, the glass shattering as the back door splintered resoundingly. Shouts in a strange Latin tongue echoed, and both men stood still, not believing this could be happening. Now self-preservation urged them to rush up the stairs for one of the bedrooms.

"Quick, before they find us," John shouted and led the way.

They had scarcely locked themselves in when they heard the sound of heavy feet rushing up the stairs and the shouts as strong shoulders were thrown against the door. Cracks appeared as more weight was applied and the door began to give. Arthur looked around and saw his suitcase. From inside the case he grabbed an aerosol of lighter fuel. He fished out a silver cigarette lighter; John followed his example and picked up a wooden chair to wield.

The door burst open and into the room rushed two splendid Roman soldiers in full uniform, their swords drawn. They were exactly alike, even to the fiery look in their eyes. They paused for a fraction of a second, then lunged. Arthur pressed the aerosol button and fired it with his lighter. A ball of flame wrapped itself around the nearest Roman's face but there was no pause, no scream as the flames burned. The sword thrust deep into Arthur's chest and blood bubbled up into his mouth. He sank to the floor. John Tudor suffered the same fate; as he swung the chair, the arc of the sword swept across his throat and he died in a second.

Their mission completed, the two soldiers went outside and joined others who stood in a long line staring up at the black night sky. All the Roman soldiers were alike, even down to their bloodstained swords. They were waiting for something.

Eventually a giant spaceship hovered for a long time over Hadrian's Wall.

A thin claw-like hand pressed a button on an energy pack set into a complex set of controls aboard the vessel. A tremendous chain-reaction was set in train; it ran through the ranks of the Roman soldiers. As each soldier was affected, he vaporised. All around the world, the same scene was enacted. At last no soldiers were left or any human life. Only then did the spaceship land. The occupants slid down the lowered gangway to explore their recently captured territory. They flapped their wings with excitement and set out to discover more of their new planet.

***

"And so the radiation, the TETRA beams, besides killing our people, also upset the time zones. That was why we returned the clones at different times throughout history, and certainly not initially at the same time. We didn't know enough to override the TETRA radiation to bunch all the clones up into one concerted attack on Earth. But when we did learn how to do it, it was too late. The radiation became our enemy."

The elder alien drew his story to an end and waited. The reaction came as he expected: the small claw-like hand he held tugged violently but still he held on. Then some time later he felt the young Sycy acting much quieter.

"What happened after the radiation sickness? Did everybody die? What about our people? What became of them?"

"Everybody died, we used clones on the Earth dwellers, then the TETRA radiation killed our people, including your parents."

"Does the picture on Earth remain the same? Do we know?" Sycy said.

For an answer the elder alien directed her gaze to a screen display on the ceiling of the spacecraft where something, picked up by a spy camera, moved.

"It is quite interesting, I think."

"What is it? That black creature."

"It's a monkey holding a wheel. Ah. Evolution again, but this time faster."

Surreal Glitter

Pippa Lewis fingered her neck, something made her uncomfortable but she shook off the feeling.

As she stood there, her eyes stayed fixed on the Bluewater necklace. The blue sapphire suggested romance to the millions of fans, around the world, who adored Beau Geste. Of course, she didn't own the original one though it went by the same name. Bluewater also happened to be an excellent choice of name for the diamond company that sold the stone. And far from being in keeping with the mystery surrounding the original Bluewater, the dealer had said nothing strange existed concerning the purchase. Rumours and curses were always created, it seemed, to generate interest in jewellery and to add in a little chill.

She sighed deeply; continued to lay out her blue gown on the bed. A glance at her Gucci watch showed ample time before friend Max appeared to taxi her and Anthony to the Summer Ball. She looked forward first to a soak in the bath and then the entertaining evening before her. Especially when she was going to wear the glittering Bluewater necklace.

She glanced up as Anthony entered the bedroom holding a silver tray which he put down on a table. He smiled, kissed her cheek and then handed her a glass of red wine from the tray. He raised his glass to his lips and followed her gaze.

"Such a beauty," he said. "Like you, Pippa."

Pippa nodded. She put down her wine and picked up the diamond necklace. The blue sapphire from Sri Lanka excited her with its clarity of colour and how it glittered. The blue stone gained its allure from its elegant setting below a series of expertly designed paved diamonds. The gold, the weight of the sapphire, and the heavy chain all indicated expensive jewellery. Pippa remembered when and where they discovered the Bluewater and the dealer who showed it to them.

Thinking about the sapphire brought back fond memories of romantic Paris.

***

As he sat in the office of 2030 Inc. Max glanced across at his boss, Cornelius Rothchild. The security of biological matters remained Max's responsibility. He used modern aids to prevent the company becoming a victim to industrial espionage. Max reflected on the positive vetting procedures, police records, the ID cards, the retina-recognition system, the use of cameras, mobile phones, the Internet and infrared cameras. He smiled to himself. He used other systems as well but they were not for general knowledge. Often he had a hunch.

"I'm amazed how well we are doing," Cornelius said. "And a lot of our success is due to your tight security. It seems we only have to publish our reports and somebody wants to steal a product."

Max nodded and made a note on the sheet of paper in front of him.

"Thanks, Cornelius," he said. "But four years ago, almost to the day, a genetics-terrorist managed to infiltrate our research team. This happened in spite of all our safety systems."

"I remember, but it wasn't your fault," Cornelius said. "Look at the good side; she never stole anything."

"Perhaps. But I'm still not happy with the incident. We guessed with her security clearance she seized the opportunity to look at our R&D files. I still wonder what she looked at and what damage she did, if any. Not knowing worries me a lot. I always like to know. When we discovered her true identity she fled immediately."

Four years ago, Carol Nugent, a bio graduate from Detroit joined 2030 Inc. Unknown to Max, BioTech Consolidated recruited her to check on 2030 Inc. products. For a short period she gained access to a number of clinical trial files. Then Max got a tip-off about her.

Naturally Max checked everything Carol might have looked at, especially the clinical trials for the product BS72. Immediately a quantity of powders, pills, and tablets were put on hold or destroyed pending investigation. Cornelius agreed with the precaution as the product got replaced.

But a question mark hung over batch BS72, the anti-ageing commodity. All research papers had been published; only the clinical trials remained before the launch onto the world markets. So far two volunteers had tried the BS72 before Carol's cover got blown. One was Linda Johnson, who'd since died in a motor accident. The other was Pippa Lewis.

Both volunteers had taken the BS72 powder with excellent results, as photographs showed. But what worried Max was whether Carol had done something to the BS72 powder samples before it had been given to Linda and Pippa.

***

Pippa Lewis looked gorgeous. At fifty she still had had a svelte figure. Now at fifty-four she still displayed the same shape and her face remained free of lines. In four years Pippa's looks remained an example of perfection.

Pippa often thought about her luck in volunteering to test the 2030 product. Four years ago she took the powder and loved the way it all worked out. Every year 2030 Inc. arranged photographs with favourable results. Her smile widened as she looked at Anthony and at the wisps of silvery hair around his temples. Anthony's paunch also got her attention. She liked to think it resulted from her special cooking recipes.

She cast her mind back to four years ago when she'd given birth to twins. Unfortunately there had been complications as the twins were stillborn. Pippa never fully recovered from the experience and she often blamed the loss of the twins on her age at the time.

Anthony had been kind; he distracted her by booking a holiday in Paris, the city of love. They might have gone there a married couple in their fifties wearing their neat clothes but they'd both decided on the magic of change.

Pippa threw away her tweeds and dyed her hair red, pulled it back into a ponytail and invested in a striped shirt. Her pink jeans set off the image she wanted, so did the open-toed sandals and the bag of lemons she carried in a string bag for the colour effect. Sometimes she put on dark sunglasses to look seductive, like a film star.

Anthony for his part donned a pair of baggy trousers with a navy blue shirt. A broad leather belt kept the trousers in place and around his neck he wore a knotted red handkerchief. He grew a beard and now wore a French beret set at a jaunty angle.

The change in dress and attitude worked wonders for both of them, especially Pippa. Anthony too enjoyed his Parisian looks and even loved being mistaken for an artist. He put it down to carrying an open bottle of wine or the two paintbrushes sticking out of his back pocket.

***

Pippa took BS72 powder four years ago and since then there'd been nothing adverse to report. Her delight at being chosen as a volunteer showed in the promotional photograph on the wall in Max's office. He looked again at the picture. Now he understood why women clamoured for BS72; ageing affected every woman.

BS72 hit the home market under the brand name of 'Cupid'. Already it generated much interest from abroad. In China the women copied the West, using cosmetic surgery to stay young. And then 'Cupid' or BS72 came onto the market.

Max grinned to himself. More customers meant more security needs and more work for him. And he liked it that way. He removed a security file from a cabinet in his office and started to read.

He read with interest the report he'd written on Carol Nugent four years previously. Max thought she may well have doctored the then trial product BS72. It was indeed lucky only two volunteers tried the product. One was now dead and the other, Pippa, showed no ill effects.

Max removed some specific photos from the file. Over the years he had become friendly with Pippa and her husband Anthony. In the pictures Max noted how good she looked at fifty-four. He also let his gaze linger on the blue sapphire necklace she wore. He remembered her story of the Bluewater, bought as a present by Anthony after the twins died at birth. The sapphire and Paris created an image of romance and he was happy for them knowing the tragedy behind the story of the stillborn twins.

***

The man in the well-cut Yves Saint Laurent suit approached their table as they sat at the cafe watching life on the street of Paris. Anthony and Pippa looked up into his tanned face; clearly he'd spent many hours in the sun.

"I'm Seb Morriss," the man drawled as he handed over a business card. "I heard you talking about the Bluewater, like in the book *Beau*

Geste. You can see I'm American but I've also been in the Foreign Legion. Sure the story of 'Beau' is so romantic. But the Bluewater, that features in *Beau Geste*, is pure fiction. What is true, however, is a fabulous blue sapphire from Sri Lanka that my company buys from a designer in Israel. This designer creates a small number of these necklaces each year and we buy every one. Here is a photograph and all the other details including the price.

"The sapphire is also called the Bluewater and is the same name of the company for which I work. I've been in the in the gem business for seven years. If you are interested in buying jewellery then contact me. You've already got my card and I'm on the Internet. I'm off to the diamond centre in Israel but I'll be back in America in two months time. Maybe you'd like to telephone me. No obligation. Enjoy your holiday."

"Thanks," Anthony said. He shook hands. "Tell me, in the book there is a lot of bad luck concerning the owners of the Bluewater, so does it come with a curse?"

Seb Morriss laughed and his eyes lit up.

"All gems do," he said. "I could kid you the Bluewater has a curse on it but I'd be wrong. The curses are an invention put on to keep the prices high. And to add mystery like the curse that goes with the tomb of King Tutankhamun. Didn't you know that?"

***

Pippa and Anthony became excited with the thought of owning a Bluewater necklace. Now they experienced Paris in a new light; it seemed vibrant, more alive and so romantic.

From their hotel base they travelled each day on sightseeing tours. They drank wine, often seeking out a new cafe in the city. Sometimes they'd search for a special place. They tasted the food from Thài restaurants and compared it with American cooking. They went to the top of the Eiffel tower, walked in the Champ de Mars and rode the Metro. They loved the experience and knew they'd remember it for a long time.

When they returned to America after their wonderful holiday they turned their thoughts to the Bluewater. A few months later they contacted the American and got the chance to handle the necklace. They bought it. From then on Pippa's world revolved around the blue sapphire necklace. It grabbed her complete attention.

"The Bluewater suits you," Seb Morriss said. He smiled. "Now here are some ownership details I need to go through with you."

***

Max pushed the doorbell and waited for a couple of minutes. Nobody came. He rang again. While he waited this time he straightened his black tie and checked his evening dress.

"Ready? I've come to take you and Pippa to the ball," Max said as Anthony opened the door. Anthony let him in. It was then Max noticed the expression on his friend's face. He saw the twisted lips; the lines running across his forehead and the way his eyes stared. "What's wrong? You look terrible. Where's Pippa?"

Anthony wore his evening suit, though his shirt lacked a black tie. Max noted the trembling shoulders, the way he fiddled with an empty jewellery box. Clearly Anthony was worried. Once they sat down Max spoke again. "Where's Pippa?"

Anthony rolled his eyes first then fixed them on the box in his hand.

"I don't know...where she is," Anthony said. "I've looked for over fifteen minutes…and I'm scared."

Max scanned Anthony's face. He got up quickly and went into the kitchen. He returned with a glass of water and gave it to Anthony to drink. Max sat down.

"Slowly now. Start at the beginning," Max said quietly. "Tell me everything, so I can help."

The water and the kind words helped Anthony to relax a fraction. He started to tell Max his story.

"We were in the bedroom," Anthony said. "Enjoying a glass of wine. I was already almost dressed so I left Pippa alone to get ready. There seemed to be plenty of time but you know what women are like with make-up, lip-gloss and all sorts of things. I didn't mind a quiet break; it gave me a chance to catch up on sport on the television.

"About twenty minutes later, I went into the bedroom. Her dress, her shoes and her handbag still lay on the bed. I checked the bathroom but she wasn't there. The bath hadn't even been used. It was really strange, as I know Pippa said she'd have a bath before getting dressed. The towels still hung on the rack. Unused.

"I shouted for her but nothing. I've checked every room in the house, I've even gone through the basement and the garage. But my

Pippa has disappeared. I'm scared in case she's been kidnapped."

"Why? Why do you say kidnapped?" Max asked gently.

"She's gone and the necklace has gone. Somebody grabbed her before she got a chance to have a bath. It must have been minutes after I left her." Anthony glanced at the empty glass still in his hand. He put it down.

"Everything is a possibility but let's go through the house together and see if we can find her."

Five minutes later Max confirmed he could find no sign of Pippa.

"Perhaps she went out," Max said. "Maybe you didn't notice."

Anthony shook his head. "I don't think so. I heard her in the bedroom singing some song. Then her singing stopped. I never saw her again. I'd have seen her if she'd tried to get past me."

"OK," Max said. He got up quickly and checked the bedroom. It was empty. He left the door open and returned to sit down facing Anthony. He checked to see if what Anthony said was true about watching the bedroom door.

"Let me make a call. I'm, kind of puzzled. I need some help on this one," Max said. He telephoned the police and then called Cornelius on his mobile.

When he finished his phone calls, Max heard something move. It dropped right into Anthony's lap. As it landed, it immediately crawled towards his face. Anthony gasped and half rose in his seat to sink back as the chameleon crawled up his body. His cry of anguish followed as his eyes latched onto those of the creature. Max saw Anthony's face change to a deathly pale colour. Anthony's lips quivered, his whole body shook as he gasped.

Max's eyes went first from the creature to the high curtain from where it had launched itself and back to it. He watched fascinated by the changing colour of the skin and the way its eyes opened wide and it looked terrified.

In a fraction of a second realisation hit Max when he caught the surreal glitter of diamonds around the chameleon's neck. Anthony too saw the necklace and gasped in disbelief.

The Bluewater around the agitated creature's neck stunned both men. Max stared and grabbed his mobile. Anthony sobbed.

"The curse. Oh my God. Pippa," Anthony said. "The curse – it's true. The man lied. He lied."

Max swore. He swore again. In the distance he heard sirens. He was aware he knew nothing about curses, especially fictional ones.

"Carol Nugent," Max swore. "Bitch. Bitch! Carol, you really did it this time!" And he knew he was right about the genetics terrorist.

The Cursed Dragon Egg

Jarge Benson took his seat on the platform beside various members of the Rotary, British Legion and Burma Star organizations. The staged event tonight was intended to raise money for local deserving causes, and was attended by over two hundred guests. He looked around, nodding to familiar faces. Now with dinner over, as entertainment, Jarge volunteered to demonstrate his famous 'mind magic' skills. His offer to guess the amount in the collection box could be the highlight of the memorable evening. A buzz of pure excitement ran through the interested audience.

For weeks before tonight's event, all money collected ended up inside a large envelope. It was next sealed inside a cardboard box and deposited with the Lloyds Bank Manager, Roy Tilley. Only he knew how much money was inside the box.

People speculated on the total collected. But in view of the many donations pouring in, it seemed a daunting task, hence the interest of the audience as they waited to see how Jarge would do. They remembered reading something in the *Oxford Mail* about a similar event.

The cardboard box stood on a table in front of Jarge. The hall went quite quiet as he picked it up. As he did so his eyes darted tentatively into the faces of his audience. He seemed to be looking for inspiration, until finally his gaze rested on the face of the Master of Ceremonies. With a smile he sat down to scribble a figure on to a piece of paper. In silence Jarge folded the paper; passed it to Grant Cockburn, MC.

"Ladies and gentlemen, now has come the time to see how much our efforts have raised in the past few weeks. How much money are we talking about? I don't know, but for a bit of fun our local celebrity, Jarge Benson, has offered to take a guess. There are no prizes to hand out for getting it right, but then this is a charity event. Now here in my hand is the amount quoted by Jarge Benson.

"For newcomers, Jarge is a well-travelled man who has a knack for the mysterious. He once lived in a temple with Buddhist monks in Tibet learning meditation and psychology skills. He also has an extensive knowledge of dragon folklore. Using his 'mind magic,' he will guess how much money is in the box. Ladies and gentlemen…Jarge Benson."

The audience noticed Jarge as a man of about sixty years old, his black hair shot with grey. They saw his weather-beaten face and those twinkling blue eyes keen enough to focus on life's interesting details. He related well to people thus making himself a extremely popular man; his bouncy nature was enough to give the appearance he was younger than his age. Everyone remembered with awe his famous interview by gorgeous presenter May Shervan. At the HTV interview, Jarge talked about his travels in Tibet and China.

"Friends," Jarge said, "there are two thousand nine hundred and fifty pounds in the box." He paused for a second to wipe his forehead. "I hope I'm correct…but let me tell you, I suspect something strange might happen tonight. I feel it in my bones."

The figure was chalked up on a large blackboard: £ 2,950.

Grant Cockburn opened the cardboard box to extract a slip of paper quoting an exact total. In silence he chalked up £2,975. Jarge was out by £25.

The audience gasped.

"Well, guess I got it wrong," Jarge admitted. "But remember what I said a few minutes ago, I'd like Roy to count out the money and tell us the real total."

Minutes later, Roy Tilley counted all the notes and drew a large circle around Jarge's figure of £2,950. It seemed Jarge did get it right after all. The audience clapped with delight.

"I'm puzzled," Jarge said, "how there should be a difference of twenty-five pounds between the money paid in and the amount actually in the box. Where did the twenty-five pounds go? Roy, do check, is there anything else in the box?"

The Lloyds Bank Manager looked concerned at the discrepancy. He shrugged as he dropped two spotted black and white pebbles onto the table.

"Only these two things."

Jarge's face was serious as he examined one of the pebbles. He took out a handkerchief and rubbed hard at the pebble but it wasn't like a bird's egg. It felt lighter. He wrapped it up and slipped it into his pocket to examine at a later date.

"I don't understand. What is this thing, this spotted pebble? Does anybody know?" Jarge asked. He had now picked up the second pebble to show to the audience.

At the back of the hall, a chair scraped, and an old Indian man shuffled his way down the central passageway of the hall. Two hundred pairs of eyes followed every movement the Indian made. They all watched in silence as he climbed the steps onto the platform.

The elderly man, in evening dress, looked distinguished, his dark complexion contrasted by the silver showing at his temples.

"Heck, Rama I haven't seen you for some time." Jarge welcomed the Indian. "But you look so well, guess it must be all that food your wife cooks for you. And are you still interested in cricket?"

Rama smiled back and extended his hand. Jarge noted several gold rings on the Indian's fingers as they shook hands. He also noted the worry lines running across Rama's forehead. The Indian seemed to be under a great deal of tension. Jarge put it down to being in front of such a daunting crowd.

The Indian's face twisted with a smile as he took the pebble from Jarge. He held it aloft so all could see the object in his hand. Jarge sat down, but carried on listening and watching. It was good to meet up with an old friend like Rama Singh.

"My name is Rama Singh and I've lived here over thirty years. I was once the manager of the Taj Mahal restaurant in London Street. Now the way I see it this dragon egg is to blame," Rama said dramatically.

The audience shuffled in their seats. They wanted to know more.

"Make sure you remember this," Rama continued. He paused to show the dragon egg to the crowds. "Be scared if you find it."

Rama paused to clear his throat.

"Many years ago in Calcutta, when I worked as a railway consultant I first saw a dragon egg. I travelled a lot and met many interesting people. In particular I made friends with Harry, a medical student living in Ripon Street.

"When we went out some evenings, it soon became apparent Harry always had more money than me. He would never let me pay my share of anything.

"We always went to expensive places to meet the girls and Harry knew them all. They loved Harry and all his money.

"I remember one day as we entered Raffles, a select restaurant in Calcutta, the manager seemed disturbed by our presence. I thought it strange, so I tried to find why he was so tense. He explained all right, but his words intrigued me.

" 'Sir,' the manager told me, 'every time your friend visits here something odd happens. When we cash up, money is missing and in its place a spotted pebble.'

"I neglected to give his words more thought, otherwise I might have wised up to the scourge of the dragon egg. As it was, I got embarrassed with Harry paying for everything. So when a new contract cropped up, I took off to Bombay, glad to leave him behind.

"You see, I discovered wherever the spotted pebble appears you would find a dragon keeper. I guess such a person has signed a deal with a dragon.

"Remember the companions of witches and vampires? They got paid to look after their masters. Here the reward is maybe a dragon egg.

"Any money spent changed into a dragon egg. It would then turn up in a cash till."

Rama paused once more to stare at his audience.

"Now some five months later I was on a train to Calcutta when a terrified passenger dragged me along the corridor to another compartment. But before I could ask questions he disappeared, leaving me to face the unknown.

"I shrugged my shoulders and went in to find a terrible mess: the walls were covered in blood marks, the ceiling splattered. On the floor was a moaning bundle of torn clothes: a man, I guessed.

"Taking a hanky out, I wiped my hands. The door handles were smeared with blood. As I turned the body over with my foot, blood streaked my clean white trousers. The man groaned. I wiped his face and gasped…it was Harry.

" 'Who did this?' I quizzed him. Harry opened his eyes and looked at me. His eyes darted about in terror, as if trying to locate some item or thing behind me.

" 'It was…' he croaked. 'We had a pact. Now it's time. No escape …time to collect. The dragon's coming back. The egg…got to get rid of it. Look! Look! Get it away from my hand. Away!'

"He opened his hand showing me the spotted pebble or dragon egg, the same as this one. I watched in fascination as he threw it down on the floor a few times. But it always returned to his hand. Each time it happened Harry became more agitated. It was bizarre, especially knowing a dragon was out there ready to collect its dues."

Rama Singh paused and looked around him. A glance confirmed the audience hung on his every word.

"When Harry said 'dragon' I guessed at Lucifer. His asking for water to drink was the excuse I needed. I shot off eager to help, but also glad to get away. I hadn't gone far when there was a *whoomph*. A blazing fireball filled the compartment with Harry still inside it.

"I next heard the terrifying roar of a wild beast. I knew the sound of most wild animals, but this belonged to some creature I could not recognise. The depth and the rawness of the noise scared me enough to flee.

"There was nothing I could do, so I let the police and firemen take over. Later, I noticed the strong smell of sulphur. It confirmed to me Harry had indeed dabbled in the occult. From what he said, I guessed he'd sold his soul to a devil-dragon. Perhaps that was why he'd always been so wealthy.

"Now I can only hazard a guess the person or persons who donated twenty-five pounds to charity are involved with the dragon occult. All I'm going to do is to get rid of this egg as best I can, for our safety."

Rama went silent for a long time. The pause was agonizing. Then after a moment of deliberation he threw the dragon egg at the wall to the left of the stage.

"May God have mercy on their soul!" he cried.

People heard the crack as the dragon egg hit the wall. Yet two hundred pairs of eyes failed to see where it went after striking the wall. The audience reacted nervously by jumping to their feet; looked around. The atmosphere in the hall was electrifying as the audience waited…waited…mouths open…eyes rolling…for the inexplicable to happen.

Grant Cockburn screamed. A fireball hit the stage and filled the hall with smoke and flames. As the horrified audience watched, a man dashed around on the platform, his evening dress ablaze. His screams of agony filled the hall as flames engulfed him. Chairs got knocked over, women screamed as the man ran in blind panic. In his desperate state the man fell off the platform. Immediately helpers attempted to cover him with coats to put out the flames. The extinguishers used on the flames came too late. Grant Cockburn, the MC, died. His death pointed to him being both a victim and servant of the dragon egg.

But even as the shocked crowd watched, they experienced the strong smell of sulphur surging through the hall. It was strong enough to make them cough. Rama's chilling words came to mind.

The sound of sirens bugled away in the distance as the ambulance headed for the hall.

Jarge got down from the platform and walked slowly to where the body of Grant Cockburn lay. With each step he took he felt another notch of fear. Everybody watched. He knelt beside the burnt body and picked up Grant's right hand. Those standing nearby gasped at what they saw – the dragon egg was attached, like a limpet mine, to his hand. They shivered expressively as they saw it was still burning.

Later the police discovered for themselves the same dragon egg fixed as if by glue to Grant's palm. They were puzzled by their find, and at a loss for a logical explanation. Naturally, the Thames Valley Police spoke to witnesses, including Jarge Benson and Rama Singh. But the investigation raised many questions. Who really was Grant Cockburn? Did the dragon egg give him his wealthy lifestyle? What persuaded him to accept the dragon egg and the curse that went with it?

The questions were endless but Jarge, Rama and the others in the Church Hall decided, in their own minds, Grant Cockburn was the man the dragon claimed as its own.

Unfortunately another burning issue remained for the Thames Valley Police to solve before they could hope to close the case.

They needed to find the rich owner of the second dragon egg…man or woman…who could say?

Only The Best

If only they had shot me at dawn.

I'd be the hero looking into the camera, my thoughts on a brave new world; altruistic ideology I guess. I could do that. This Colombian agent would do anything to stay alive.

How is it luck often tilts the equation, determining the strange pattern of life when 'if only' becomes a mumbling, a chant, the ultimate mantra, nay, a sad prayer on the lips of this condemned man? Mind you, I die in the next three minutes. No crisp breeze on my forehead or the dawn twitter of songbirds in my ears, rather death tied to iron rings in the wall. Now at midday the temperature rockets, the dust chokes and I crave more red Burgos wine.

The soldiers, my black hood, the scary silence mean one thing: the bullet. As the minutes tick by, I torture myself with cruel thoughts, knowing I'm to blame. Me? Unlucky me? Absolutely.

My mind flips back in time…

***

Let me bend your ear before you dare judge. Listen well; think of your family in case it happens to you. Pray to your God. I do.

A pure love of Colombia flows through my veins like mountain streams, generating the tingle, the sparkle, the zest for life. It will always be there. How I bless my gift of languages, my knack of using disguise and the skill of being so streetwise. I'm acknowledged as the best secret agent in my time. But poverty and the urge to help my country really puts fire in my soul. From the gutter to the stars is some jump, especially for this one-time urchin.

Life seemed good. Too good, until the fateful day eighteen months ago when General Cauca outlined my next mission.

***

"Yes, Paulo, the country we watch uses *Diablo* in army ciphers. You must infiltrate, get close to the action. Read this. It's for background information." The General handed me several sheets of paper to read. I took them and glanced at the titles then put them to one side. "Intelligence is everything. Keep reading."

The General picked up a glass of red wine and drank it quickly. He belched and laid a hand over his bulging stomach. I could only guess his ulcer was playing him up once more. "I still look after your wife, for you. Remember?" The General twisted his mouth into a smile. As soon as he mentioned my Magdalena I really started to listen. How could I know what he was going to say next? What threat had he in mind? I only expected him to work me harder as he always seemed to do. "Trust me." He looked at me and gave me an odd sideways glance. "Why are you so quiet? Don't you have anything to say?"

"Yes. Plenty, General, but you don't listen."

"So, what do you want to say? You want me to stop looking after your Magdalena? Is that it? Where would she be without the drugs? Cancer is a killer, you know."

"OK. So I owe you. No need to rub it in. I've looked at these sheets. I know what you want. I'll do my duty. I owe you and my Magdalena that much."

The General's face softened. He drank more wine.

"So we understand each other. Good luck and don't get shot, will you? Ha! Ha!"

As he laughed at his own joke I noticed how he filled his tailor-made uniform. Fat. One of his shirt buttons was missing, but I didn't tell him.

General Cauca used me. I knew that but I depended on him. It was simple: if I fluffed my part he always threatened to stop the drugs keeping Magdalena alive. I felt like a dummy in a luckless situation. But always when I went on a mission I dreaded the possibility that a man like General Cauca, who worshipped money, might defect to the enemy.

***

I obeyed the General's instructions and in doing so I followed my love of horses; I joined the Cavalry progressing through the ranks. In any exercise or skirmish I imagined myself killing the fat General Cauca.

Such was my fire-hot enthusiasm it drew attention; my name entered the secret *Diablo* file. Controller Juan E. Brossa faced me for the interview.

Juan sat at his desk, looking up at my six-foot frame, his black hair greased flat to his scalp, his lackluster eyes staring through me. A taste in expensive grey suits matched the rich Havana cigars he smoked. What else can I tell you about him? Nothing, except he displayed no warmth, only the quiet supercilious element of power; he held my life in his hands. I didn't like him.

My tension increased as he flicked through my file. I moaned about the heat and drank more water. My heart beat faster as I saw the cryptic word *Diablo* written in pencil on a top sheet. Then I listened to the man speak in Spanish. I couldn't quite place the region but his Spanish was good.

"Paulo Basques, we like your application. Good. Your English is perfect. It is one reason we want you to start training right now. The project we have in mind is of the utmost importance because it will create havoc amongst our enemies. But there is something you need to be fully aware. We shoot you if you fail. Like this. Our beloved General insists we only get the best."

With the skill of a trained assassin Juan pointed his revolver at my head, then a smile danced across his pencil-thin lips.

"So far there has been no risk of the enemy knowing of our plans and that is how we like to keep it.

"What we ask is for you to serve your country. It is quite easy. We will train you. We will look after you. Even provide you with a new name. Miguel sounds a good name for you. So shall we go for that? Miguel? What do you say?"

Juan, this devil in a grey suit, waited for my answer. Like laser probes, his black eyes darted about scanning my face. But self-preservation forced me to conceal my emotions. My smile back at him was faint: I was hoping to give the impression of a shocked man, yet one determined to serve 'my' country. Casually I fingered the medal of St. Christopher around my neck.

My lack of choice meant I accepted what was offered because of Magdalena. I guess my interview with Juan E. Brossa was quite successful.

***

The following weeks saw me catapulted into the espionage scenario as I joined others at a secret camp. Appearing smart might have drawn too much attention so I steered towards the middle line, after all, I was thinking of the consequences to Magdalena should I fail.

My steady progress continued until that day I decoded a special message. Easy. I did decoding all the time. Yet moments later I felt the body blow. What I read made my throat feel as dry as a bone. My legs shook as I stood up.

"It can't be true."

"No mistake, Miguel. You fail, so we shoot you. Remember, 'only the best'."

I nearly choked. Ha! Shoot me? Me, the best secret agent in Colombia?

Two frightened faces looked at me from within the prison cell as I entered it. I recognized them from my training course. So they too were failures and faced death. But nothing could halt the incessant babbling of their innocence. Psychologically and physically the men were broken. Mind you, I felt like them on the inside but for me there was nothing to say. How could I let on I was the best spy in Colombia? If I did, I faced certain death. No, I could only keep my mouth shut, face the old threat of a firing squad and pray.

***

The red Burgos wine offered a little relief; it was so rough and strong. The salty bread I tore off in strips and drank with the wine. Of course the salt encouraged my thirst, so I drank more wine trying to drown my sorrow, to stop the pain in my head.

As I waited, I thought about Magdalena and what General Cauca threatened. All my old worries resurfaced. To block out those emotions my mind skipped back in time, to places where I'd been happy. I remembered locations in Colombia and Europe.

When a child I remember wandering outside in the hot noonday sun to show my friends a piece of bread. What a mistake! Out of the sky dropped a black shadow and the thing - a black hawk - grabbed the bread in its talons and made off. I never forgot the lesson. Never show off. I remembered my hot tears and the laughter of those who watched the incident. Hunger is a good teacher.

In Colombia I came close to nature and enjoyed early morning walks with dew still on the grass, the joy of seeing spiders' webs and the rain. When you are about to die, it's amazing what you value most…Only the best know the meaning of 'bittersweet'.

I thought about my wife Magdalena; her anguish on hearing of my death. I would never say my last goodbye, to feel the softness of her skin or caress her as I kissed those red lips. I imagined how she would stand, arms folded, eyes staring blankly at the sky, thinking only of the man snatched from her, a man whose love was denied her for the rest of her days. Tears filled my eyes. Unashamedly I wiped my face with the sleeve of my shirt. Believe me, my friend, this is rock bottom.

Prayers tripped off my lips as I waited, but was it too late? Memories came to mind of the Camargue in France when an eighty-year-old peasant spoke about the 'person' walking alongside me. Yet I knew I was alone. The peasant saw my 'dear companion', I guessed. Now I needed help from anywhere. Even a guardian angel would suit me.

***

I moved restlessly about the cell like a caged animal. Every piece of the cell came under my scrutiny. Pencilled notes drew my attention, all from other prisoners now dead and gone. The line 'Beware of Friend: Beware of Foe' on a wall was enough to catch my attention.

My thoughts slipped into another gear. Now I dreamed of the reason why I should not be shot. Should or could this all be a big bluff? The army psycho chaps got up to all sorts of mean tricks. Could this be one? Tiredness dictated I didn't need or want to know more. Oh, Magdalena.

As I nurtured these thoughts, my cellmates flipped their lids. But their calls for mercy to the stoic guards went unheeded.

"Please, please don't kill me. It's a mistake. I am Angelo." I listened to their confessions; they blew their cover telling the guards, revealing their true identity. They clearly weren't trained enough, like me a good secret agent, to know the danger of revealing all.

Nothing could calm the two men. They babbled constantly. They drank excessive amounts of wine provided to loosen their tongues. They got sick. Nobody cleaned the mess and still they babbled on.

Their voices pleaded but nobody listened. I could do nothing except turn away and keep quiet. Escape was impossible and I knew it. Against this grim tapestry, I heard the sweet call of a bird to its mate. My thoughts were on Magdalena once more.

My two course companions left the cell an hour later dragging their legs. I could still smell the vomit. I spent my wretched time wondering on their fate. Minutes passed until the staccato shots and the brief echo. Now it was my turn. A church bell tolled.

***

In my mind's eye I saw a statue of the Blessed Virgin enthroned in a lattice of gold and silver robes. I also saw poor people praying at her feet, an animation in their faces; such faith kept the women and children together to survive.

The black hood gave me a hot head. The sweat soaked my shirt, burning my eyes. Scared, whilst my life ticked away. In spite of the background noises I sensed a stillness, the lull before the storm. Too late for God to help me…

The rifles cracked once followed by the long echo. Dead? Was I to sleep forever?

A hand snatched off my black hood and I looked into the face of Juan E. Brossa, the devil in grey. His eyes sparkled as he fixed me with his gaze. He was laughing. Laughing. Laughing at my plight. I hated him. I felt as if I'd lost my soul.

Juan shouted out his good wishes in Spanish.

"Congratulations, Miguel, you passed our surprise test in excellent style. Here, let me free you. As we said before we only want the best agent possible for a secret project. It seems you could be our man. My, you stayed so cool. Even under stress. We did it to test you. So, now we know you are really our man, Miguel."

Ha! They *had* played the psycho game on me. Hate welled up inside me. How many agents died because of Juan E. Brossa? The mental pain I experienced demanded vengeance.

***

Juan's face broke into a smile as he lit his long cigar. While walking beside me he pointed at the rifles the neat soldiers carried. It was such a casual gesture. And as I walked my face was a mask to hide my thoughts. I really felt like killing him but then I thought my Magdalena would suffer if I died. She needed those drugs.

Again that bird singing in the background captured my attention, its song told of freedom. Yet in the next second a woman screamed under torture from close by. Too surreal for me, especially when next I heard the persistent sound of a baby crying. I loved children. Guess I've never been so close to death.

We walked on. The hot air carried the aroma of cooking from a nearby kitchen. Immediately images crowded into my mind. Images I cherished when I thought of my wife. I longed for my Magdalena, the feel of her soft skin on my rough cheeks, the fragrance of her hair. Her dark eyes and sensuous body always made her my wife and lover.

Thorny bushes and weeds flanked the bricked archway leading out of the courtyard. Deeply rooted vines tied against the walls soared to the heavens. I looked at the dark patches on some walls, the evidence of a gory past. Few things change but if they shot me at dawn I would have missed all this in the dark.

Juan E. Brossa spoke to me again in Spanish.

"They used only blanks: so you were in no danger, Miguel," Juan said. He saluted the soldiers.

My nervous wide-open smile came back at him. Soon feelings returned to my body. I walked a little shakily across the courtyard, blinking in the glaring sunlight. My watering eyes matched the lump in my throat.

But the sunlight wasn't so strong I could fail to notice the two still bodies half hidden by an old blanket in the far corner of the courtyard.

Childers

The tiny speck of virginal white against the coal-black rock caught the dragon's attention.

Carefully yet quickly, it changed direction to drop several hundred feet out of the blue June sky.

Below the beast, the bright sunlight reflected off the surface of the enormous lake, the Faringdon Mere. Besides being well-known for its size, the Mere had a chilling reputation as the 'killing fields' where Vestal Virgins died due to the ferocious actions of the local dragon.

Apprehensive watchers first noticed the tiny black dot in the sky, then followed the flames and smoke trailing from it as the dragon drew nearer. The close proximity of the dragon set in motion a chain reaction; some fainted at the sight, others hid their faces; those who worshipped pagan gods fingered tokens around their necks.

Nothing could stop the dragon once it locked onto the young female chained to the black rock. Her white robes lifted in the wind, her long yellow hair moved across her face, the terror clearly evident from the way she looked as she faced the awesome dragon.

The creature's grunt carried across the waters as it landed on the black rock. The virgin screamed. In vain, she strained at her chains, her blue eyes bulging at the dragon's approach. It advanced inch by inch with only the pleasure of the kill and the feast in its mind.

The dragon paused. It struck.

The young victim screamed once.

Immediately a deep sigh of horror escaped from the lips of the hidden watchers as everything went quiet. As the dragon ate, some continued praying. Many knew the scene from previous years when the dragon first appeared. To maintain peace a young maiden from a village nearby became an offering to the dragon. Then years later when a cool-headed cavalryman dispatched the dragon it went into the spirit world. Sometimes it emerged with a vengence on 'Childers...'

***

Edward Chadwick, Oxford University tutor, read the intriguing details of the Mere in the diary of a local historian. Since the language of the diary was updated it was easier to understand. In it he read the first description of the now non-existent lake. Nothing intrigued Edward more than the sinister role played by the lake concerning the burial rites of young children.

He was thirty-seven with brown hair and an interest in dark drab clothes. Sometimes he sported a bow tie to brighten his image. His choice of clothes changed when he met Anita. His friends smiled, knowing romance accounted for the lighter trousers he wore now and his old cords were a thing of the past, as were his pigskin shoes. His new belt and new shoes were now made of real leather.

***

"What, no children's graves? Here, let me read." Edward snatched the bit of paper from his girlfriend and assistant Anita Meile. Both enjoyed their Mortuary Studies for the Oxford University, especially when it involved the Faringdon Mere.

"Martha Binnie died 1548, aged three; Flo Mallows, 1682, seven; Bow Cowley, 1796, only five...Hell, the list goes on and on. So where are they buried?" Edward asked.

Anita Meile, a tall blonde Swedish degree student, shrugged her shoulders. Her recent finding showed no graves existed for children who died in Faringdon between 1500 and 1800.

The records puzzled Edward until he discovered an old map found in the ruins of the workhouse at the top of London Street. The Faringdon Mere dominated the map simply because of its vast size and its connection with the dead children from the workhouse. It was evident to Edward he needed help with his project: he consulted the rustic character Jarge Benson.

***

Jarge Benson was about sixty, sun-tanned with a beard, black hair shot with grey and a bouncy nature. He was active and ever helpful when it came to answering Edward's questions.

"True. The local chaps would put the bones in sacks and fill them with rocks. Then they'd drop the sacks into the Mere to save on funeral expenses. Must be thousands of dead bodies in there. Doesn't matter anymore 'cause they drained the Mere and diverted the river feeding the lake.

"I'm sure the Mere was well-known, even in Roman times, because it was used to sacrifice virgins to the dragon. Did I ever tell you about a great big black rock..."

The wealth of information Jarge supplied enabled Edward to complete his many notes. Jarge also drew Edward's attention to the writings of an interesting local man.

Benjamin, a Faringdon hangman and poet, once penned a haunting line about the lake. As a poet he wrote about the 22nd July or 'Childers': *when young 'uns gets up an gey the dance, and race against the sands o' time.*

Folklore encouraged the idea that this was the night when the dead buried in the Mere took on flesh and blood and came 'alive'. Edward was fascinated by the concept and resolved to find out more. But what puzzled him was the name 'Night of the Dragon' though more often it was called 'Childers'.

***

When Anita returned to Sweden to care for her sister injured in a car accident, Edward carried on with his work. He missed his thirty-year old helper and looked forward to her return. The months sped by during which time she sent a letter every week to update him. Edward enjoyed reading the letters but he'd really have preferred his talks with her and her company. In fact, six months passed and he wondered if he'd ever see her again.

As Edward waited for Anita to return, a new development occurred concerning the Mere. Thames Water decided to change the river so it took its former route to create a reservoir - a lake - but Edward knew it was the Faringdon Mere. The appearance of a giant black rock sticking up out of the water hinted it might be connected with some dark incident in the past. Edward accepted its new position though he was slightly puzzled as he remembered it once lying on the dried-up riverbed.

Edward's interest with the vast Mere often found him spending many long hours looking out across the waters, thinking of his beloved Anita. In her last letter she mentioned she might be returning to

England within days. Carefully Edward weighed up her words. He wondered if she might be back in time. His mind was on other things as already it was July. He was thinking of the 22nd or 'Childers'…

***

'Childers' night came. Edward took out the punt and the experience stunned him. He was not sure what to expect but this first time he encountered thousands of glittering lights. All across the surface of the Mere, Edward saw what looked like fairy lights. They disappeared after a few minutes leaving him slightly disappointed. He couldn't help but feel there was more to follow. He wrote his impressions down in a book and continued his research.

Then Anita returned from Sweden. Edward was so pleased to see her back. As they exchanged information, news and bonded again he saw sadness in her beautiful face. He kissed her gently, stroked her long blonde hair and then as he drew her closer he felt her whole body shake. She sobbed. Her whole body shook with her grief and Edward did his best to comfort her.

"Lisa. She died," Anita said. "Oh. My lovely Lisa." As she started to talk, Anita opened up a conversation in which she expressed her feeling. She told him how the letters he wrote to her kept her spirits high, especially when her mother became depressed. The six months of support from Edward were, Anita said, a debt she'd never be able to repay.

The story Anita told him about Lisa was tragic: a car hit her sister after leaving school. As a direct result of the accident, Lisa went into a coma, which killed her in the end.

"This is what I keep to remember her," Anita said. She showed Edward a photograph of her sister. Anita then told him how her sister had been cremated and the ashes buried in a family plot.

As Edward watched, Anita stiffened. She dried her tears with a tissue, then kissed him gently.

"What have you been doing while I've been away, my love?"

"I've been working on the Mere. I went across it on 'Childers'. It was so strange. I saw thousands of little lights shining above the surface of the lake. It really startled me because one minute it was night time and then the lights came on. I felt there was more to it all than just the lights. But who knows for sure. I don't even know where those lights came from. I guess I'll have to wait to next year now."

"How weird. Now tell me again," Anita insisted. "Everything. In case you've missed something. I want to come with you on the next 'Childers'."

***

In the months that followed Edward spent time going through all the data and various files he'd researched, in order to bring Anita up to date with the mysterious Mere.

But when Anita came back to England she brought new problems for Edward. There was little doubt her mind still dwelt on her sister's death and it was that which led to her suffering with depression, an illness her mother suffered from, too. To lift Anita's spirits Edward arranged a long holiday in Cornwall but the break didn't have the desired effect for which he hoped. All Edward ended up doing was watching her take the prescribed pills with the slim possibility she might get better.

Sometimes Anita smiled. Edward loved it when that happened and the way she flicked her blonde hair off her face. He remembered those days as the ones when she felt better, and assisted him with his research project. Perhaps, with a little luck, all the work might get finished on time.

Often Edward struggled on his own and then July 22nd loomed on the horizon. He mentioned the date to Anita and noted how her depression seemed to have lifted. At last he could plan with her what to do on 'Childers' when anything might happen.

***

At eleven-thirty Edward steered the punt towards the middle of the Mere. He tied it up to some branches sticking out of the water. With Anita he settled down to wait.

The minutes ticked by...Nearly midnight; Edward squeezed Anita's hand. He couldn't help noticing how restless she was and her rapid breathing.

A few minutes later thousands of tiny lights flickered around them. Though it was close to midnight the sky already looked lighter and continued to change. Then a strange feeling swept over Edward. He smelt fresh-cut grass and at the same time trees and bushes reared up out of the now past shadows. In the now daylight birds sang and on the superb green lawns children ran around as they played ball, laughed and had fun, the girls in white dresses, the boys in white shirts and shorts.

Edward and Anita watched the children at play from their concealed position behind some trees. They were disconcerted when the children all turned to stare directly at them. The children looked so 'real'. To Edward and Anita nothing ghostly existed involving these 'young uns'.

As the children stopped playing to stare at them, Anita raised her arm. Edward noticed her agitation and heard her choked cry. He turned his head and looked to where she pointed with trembling fingers, but Edward saw nothing. He looked back at Anita, saw the way her eyes were shining, how quickly she gasped, and how she tried to get the words out. There was no doubt she'd seen something and he couldn't.

"Anita. What is it? What do you see? Tell me."

Before he got a response from Anita, Edward noticed an object, a black creature appear some way off. But it approached them at some speed. He cried out in horror.

"Holy Toledo."

The creature got bigger as it approached and when it roared, flames shot from its mouth. He saw the legendary dragon but not whatever Anita saw.

"Lisa!" Anita yelled. "She's there. My Lisa." Her words shocked Edward as did the dragon that was growing in size as it got nearer.

Anita stood up in the punt. Without thinking she stepped onto the lawn. Immediately daylight disappeared and darkness reigned. Edward heard the splash she made as she fell in the water. He climbed over the side of the punt and managed to grab her as she thrashed around. Already the coldness of the water weakened him and he tried to drag Anita back to the side of the moored punt. But even as he did so flames from the dragon swept his face. The intense heat burnt his face. He cried out with the pain, aware of the spots in front of his eyes and knowing his flesh had been burnt.

Eventually the dragon attack passed. It left him still holding Anita and hanging onto the side of the punt while he endured the agony. He knew things had gone wrong for him with Anita staying so still and his eyes burning like a fire.

***

The dull gamekeeper Sidney Wickstead found Edward the next morning. He called the emergency services.

"Anita is dead. Drowned," Sidney told Edward in his rough monotone voice. "And the dragon's blinded you. I can guess how it happened. I know all about it. That's why I keep away from the Mere, especially on 'Childers'. Hard luck, mate."

Edward cried at his words, words said without any feelings.

About The Author

Cleveland is a new writer. He enjoys drama, the surreal. His work is showcased on www.LauraHird.com and spans many genres with publications around the world. *Moondust* represents his first short story collection to be followed by an adventure magical-realism serial aimed at children and adults. Look on his planned website www.ClevelandWGibson.co.uk for details of current projects on which he is working. Cleveland has trained as a Lifeguard, been a road race director amongst other things. Now he writes, is a dedicated carer, a teacher of ESOL, and is hoping to teach creative writing in historic Faringdon.

Contact link://linktitles.com?tile=641